PENGUI

UNCERTA

Clare Chambers was born in 1966, attended a school in Croydon and read English at Oxford. Her first novel, *Uncertain Terms* (Penguin, 1993), was written while she was living in New Zealand. She now lives in south London with her husband and young daughter. Her second novel, *Back Trouble*, is also published by Penguin.

CLARE CHAMBERS

UNCERTAIN TERMS

PENGUIN BOOKS

PENGUIN BOOKS

Published by the Penguin Group
Penguin Books Ltd, 27 Wrights Lane, London W8 5TZ, England
Penguin Books USA Inc., 375 Hudson Street, New York, New York 10014, USA
Penguin Books Australia Ltd, Ringwood, Victoria, Australia
Penguin Books Canada Ltd, 10 Alcorn Avenue, Toronto, Ontario, Canada M4V 3B2
Penguin Books (NZ) Ltd, 182–190 Wairau Road, Auckland 10, New Zealand

Penguin Books Ltd, Registered Offices: Harmondsworth, Middlesex, England

First published by André Deutsch 1992
Published in Penguin Books 1993
3 5 7 9 10 8 6 4 2

Printed in England by Clays Ltd, St Ives plc

To Peter

1

TWO minutes before Charlotte reached the lecture theatre, she was nearly killed by a meteorite.

She saw a flash of darkness out of the corner of her eye, and then heard the thud as it impacted into the baked mud of the playing field, which was parched and split from a fortnight without rain. Her first instinct was to look around accusingly for the launcher of the missile, expecting to see a group of schoolboys doubled up and punching each other at the thrill of a near miss. But there was nobody. She was quite alone in the middle of a cricket pitch. It was only when she examined the object, scrabbling in the dirt to excavate it from the little pockmark it had dug for itself, that she guessed what it was. It was about the size of a small fist, surprisingly spherical, and pitted like the surface of the moon. It was weighty enough, too, had she been just a few inches further to the right, to have cracked her skull, and to Charlotte's astonishment, it still emitted a ghostly warmth. Cradling it in her hands like a wounded bird, she hurried on to the lecture, glancing into the sky every few paces to check that there were no more extra-terrestrial crumbs falling towards her.

"The central paradox of the 'Romantic' period is the clash between the infinite power of the imaginative vision, and the poverty of the medium in which it had to be expressed. 'How feebly words essay / To fix one spark of beauty's heavenly ray.' That's Byron of course."

Oliver Shaw left his lecture notes on the rostrum and began strolling casually up and down, scanning the crowded theatre. It was the fourth year he had given this course of lectures and they always went down well. Another run would see him word perfect.

"The failure of language is a recurrent motif — consider Coleridge's Ancient Mariner, sucking his own blood, indulging in a brief act of cannibalism" (he was enjoying himself now) "before he can cry out. For Coleridge, of course, the imagination was a terrifying opium-induced phantasmagoria," he paused, listening complacently to the scratch of biro on paper. "He describes it as 'the fiendish crowd of shapes and thoughts that tortured me'."

A thin scruffy student with a pale, weasel-like face, slumped with his head on his arms as if unconscious, suddenly sat up at this point. Taking a stump of pencil from behind his ear, he started leafing through his volume of Coleridge and writing notes in the margin.

It was an unusually hot day for April and the lecture hall was packed with students whose scholastic enthusiasm rarely outlasted the introductory lecture, and who vanished from the English Faculty like phantoms after the first week of term. Several were wilting in the heat already, shifting about on their seats, leaving sweaty patches on the vinyl. Occasionally someone would wait until Dr Shaw was walking away, declaiming with his eyes half shut, then make a break for the door, either from boredom, claustrophobia, or a dim realisation that they were in the wrong lecture.

"Next week I'll begin by talking about the importance of Genesis and the myth of the Fall to writers of this period. I'm thinking primarily of Blake's *Songs of Innocence and Experience*, Shelley's *Prometheus Unbound* and Mrs Shelley's *Frankenstein*, and the idea of writing itself as a form of Fall, from the purity of conception to the ambiguity of the word." He glanced up at the clock. Ten minutes to go.

There was a sudden burst of noise from the group outside awaiting the eleven o'clock session, as another escapee pushed the door open. Oliver gave the departing back an icy stare and continued.

"If there's time I'll end up by looking at the theme of the imaginative vision as a form of demonic offspring – you will recall Mary Shelley's description of *Frankenstein* as her 'hideous progeny'. The works of Coleridge, too, are pregnant with similar images." He paused to allow the more alert to chortle politely. "The fertile landscape of 'Kubla Khan' with its chasm and 'fast thick pants' is a metaphor for the body labouring to bring forth its offspring, and the poet/prophet erupting into poetry." He took a swig of water.

At this point an enraptured first year, who was sitting near the back, was experiencing a failure of language of a less metaphysical nature. "My pen has run out," she whispered to her neighbour. "Can you take notes for me?" This was a superfluous request, since the girl beside her was already scribbling away in an effort to record every word that issued from the magisterial figure at the front.

Charlotte, standing on the balcony which ran along the side of the auditorium, still clutching her meteorite, was surveying the audience. She was amused to recognise on the faces of some of the female students the same expression of complete intellectual and emotional surrender which had afflicted her friend Alison during an identical lecture the year before. 'What does she see in him?' she wondered yet again, looking critically at his jumper with leather patches sewn into the elbows, and sleeves which showed too much shirt cuff, and the way he would flatten a book open with the heel of his hand until it submitted with a crack. (Alison's spine was clearly more flexible than that of *The Complete Coleridge*.)

Now he was digressing, mournfully listing the catalogue of early deaths, suicides and miscarriages which had pursued the Shelleys and their contemporaries. His voice was lowered slightly, a misty look in his blue eyes. The women around Charlotte were absent-mindedly stroking their bare arms,

3

their hands flitting to re-arrange loose strands of hair, or adjust a neckline. 'Not a dry pair of knickers in the house,' thought Charlotte contemptuously.

"I wish Roger hadn't sent Alison to Oliver Shaw for tutorials this term," the tutor for Women's Studies had confided in Charlotte, the week before Oliver finally pounced. They were sitting on her paisley sofa, half-way into Charlotte's essay. Mrs Summers, with consummate skill, had managed to guide the discussion away from Wordsworth's *Prelude* and on to sexual harassment within the university. 'How did she manage that?' Charlotte wondered with grudging admiration; there did not seem to be any obvious links. Sometimes it was an education having a tutor who enjoyed a twenty-minute excursion into the less cerebral aspects of academic life. She was sufficiently indiscreet to disclose all the newsworthy scandals, and was always ready to hint at the blinkered despotism of her head of department, Roger Lord. Her reputation for backstabbing had earned her the nick-name Brutus amongst her students.

"Oliver has only recently split up with his wife," she was saying, giving Charlotte a knowing look. "Only Roger would have sent a girl like Alison to him. You would have been a much safer choice." Charlotte wondered whether this was a compliment or an insult.

". . . but Roger positively refuses to admit that anything like that goes on. By the way, I thought your essay went well. Did we finish it?" she continued, her eyes glazing over as she tried to remember what, exactly, it had been about.

Oliver had become aware of Alison as a sexual entity before she became his tutee. He was in the Upper Reading Room of the Bodleian one afternoon, re-reading one of his own essays on Saussure and wondering whether it could be re-hashed for his new book, when he noticed he was being observed by an attractive young woman several tables away.

The library was a fiendish place for eye contact. The partitions running along the middle of the tables seemed to have been designed to encourage flirtation rather than privacy, reaching as they did to just below eye-level. Each time he looked up from his work his gaze was met by a pair of large brown eyes which would then look away, a fraction of a second too late. He tried it a few more times. He was not imagining it — she was definitely watching him. He put his head down and went back to his work.

Saussure put forward the theory that language, far from merely naming pre-existing concepts, actually creates and articulates those concepts itself; the signified does not pre-date the signifier, nor does it have an innate quality independent of the signifier. Both signifier and signified are symbiotic aspects of the sign which is itself merely an arbitrary division of a continuous linguistic-conceptual spectrum there was no doubt about it, she was very good looking indeed, and now she was standing up and taking another volume of *Neophilologus* from the shelf beside her. Slim. Long brown hair. Long brown legs. Oliver struggled to regain his concentration. Libraries always made him feel incredibly randy. And museums. The girl sat down again, staring at him from under half-lowered eyelashes. He was tempted to smile, but knew that, just as on the underground, there was a code of etiquette operating here that permitted any amount of eye-contact, provided neither party actually acknowledged it.

'Stop being such a lecherous old goat,' he told himself, angling his chair to obstruct the view, and when he looked up again at the end of the chapter, she had gone.

So he was surprised and delighted when, the following week at his first tutorial of the term, he found her sitting outside his study, a neat little essay on her knees and an eager smile on her lips. He was going to enjoy Wednesday afternoons, he decided; she promised to be wonderfully teachable.

Charlotte, for her part, had been unable to reassure Mrs Summers about Alison's propensity for being seduced. She had always suspected Alison's judgement in matters of men — falling for one's tutor was so *obvious*. Alison was also too optimistic; too eager to mistake lust for genuine affection. (For Charlotte the two rarely coincided.) In addition, Charlotte had been a constant and bemused witness to Alison's escalating interest in Oliver; her regular detours past his college, her slavish attendance at even the most obscure of his lectures, and finally, once she became one of his pupils, her obsessive preparations for every tutorial.

"What shall I wear?" she wailed, rifling through her wardrobe seeking the one perfect outfit that would make her look lovely, intelligent - without - being - in - any - way - threatening, inaccessible and available all at the same time. She pulled out a white summer dress and held it against herself. Charlotte, sitting on the window seat eating a kebab (Alison had abstained, not wanting to smell of garlic), felt slightly disgusted at the sight of her friend tricking herself out like a sacrificial virgin, but said nothing.

Alison ironed the dress on a pillow case on the floor, put it on, took one look at Charlotte's expression and changed back into jeans. Then she spent the next half-hour arranging and re-arranging her hair, before giving up and leaving it loose.

"I don't want to look as if I'm trying too hard — he mustn't think I'm chasing him," were her last words.

Charlotte had never met anyone who made passivity seem so gruelling.

And then there was the endless analysis.

"He suggested I read Hazlitt's *Liber Amoris*. Do you think that's a good or a bad sign?"

"He lent me his copy of *Don Juan* and it has his address in the front. He must have intended me to see it."

And "What has he written on my essay? I can't read his handwriting — something about wonderful."

Charlotte took the page from her and pulled a face at his spidery scribble. "It says 'wandering', not 'wonderful'.

6

'Wandering into the abstract at times, but never less than perceptive,'" she read, deciphering slowly. This was another mark against him. She always distrusted people with illegible writing. There was something furtive and ungenerous about it; an obstructive element of power play seemed to be involved. Her own writing was fat, round and utterly candid. If she made a spelling error it was there for all to see.

Alison was still dissecting Oliver's annotations to her work.

"He seems to have been *about* to write 'wonderful'," she insisted. "He's changed the 'o' to an 'a' and the 'ing' has come through on to the page below, as if he was pressing harder."

"Don't you think you might be reading too much into all this?" Charlotte suggested.

"But we're students of literature. We're supposed to be sensitive to ambiguity."

And so, in spite of the combined vigilance of Charlotte and Mrs Summers, the inevitable had happened.

It had been a rare, warm day in the middle of term, and Oliver had spent the morning clearing all his wife's remaining belongings into garden refuse bags and putting them in the attic. In a moment of inspired malice, he kept back a pair of fringed cowboy boots which he had always hated, and gave them to Beckford the dalmatian, who chewed them joyfully. It was now six weeks since she had left, taking as much as she could fit in the Volvo. Even that had been a deliberate gesture.

"You can't take that . . ." he had protested, as she loaded her suitcases into the boot.

"Watch me," she said through clenched teeth. "For two years you've driven this and left me to use that useless heap of tin." She aimed a vicious kick at the mini, which was parked behind, shabby and freckled with rust like an old dog. "I've had more AA men than you've had hot dinners."

'I've been lucky to get one of those lately,' Oliver thought.

At first he had not been able to face sorting out the rest

of her personal items, half hoping she would change her mind and come back. It was not that he loved her any more. The venom of their final argument had left him quite numb, but he could not get used to the eerie silence of the house. Even rows had been a sign of life. Their neighbours may have called the police once during one of their more animated exchanges, but he still believed a marriage was technically a success, provided both partners lived under the same roof.

By now it was evident that she had no intention of returning, other than to collect her last few remnants. It amazed him how thoroughly the removal of one carload of familiar possessions had managed to bleach the house of all trace of warmth and personality. He had not been mistaken about the air of menace in her tone when she promised to split everything down the middle. She had done so with surgical precision, leaving him feeling like an amputee, with the second half of a box set of *Der Ring*, and the P–Z volume of the *Compact Oxford Dictionary*.

"You had a lucky escape," he said to the dog.

He had a few minutes to spare before his tutorial with Alison, and decided to look in the bookshop. He was idly browsing through the new publications in the Literary Criticism department when he noticed that the girl next to him had picked up his own book, *The Last Days of the Novel*. She had long shiny blonde hair and her lips were coated with what looked like a thin layer of redcurrant jelly. Oliver swelled. It was nice to be picked up — even by proxy.

"Isn't this on your reading list?" she called out, waving it at her companion, who was standing some way off.

"Oh God no," the girl replied in a penetrating voice. "Nobody reads that any more."

Mortified, Oliver plunged out of the shop. *The Last Days of the Novel* had been a minor classic eighteen years before, when he was a brilliant young post-graduate. Wittily and persuasively, he had predicted the demise and extinction of an entire literary form. The sequel, *The Last Days of the Critic*, was taking considerably longer. The idea of a critical essay denouncing criticism — a work which would have to invalidate itself systematically as it proceeded — at first intoxicated him. As the monumental futility of the whole task began to dawn on him, his enthusiasm had turned to exasperation. The whole project had finally been shelved in favour of a commissioned introduction to George Herbert, even though he knew it did not have quite the same potential for shaking the academic establishment to its foundations.

Oliver arrived at the tutorial, his ego in tatters, as if nothing but an incarnation of uncritical adoration could restore him to a sense of his own greatness. And there she sat, in a shaft of dusty light, in a white dress, in his study, infatuated.

The lecture was over. Oliver Shaw swept his books off the rostrum and strode out. Charlotte allowed herself to be carried along by the crowd towards the exit. In the car park Alison was leaning against her bicycle chatting to Oliver. He gave Charlotte a nod as she approached, and then sauntered off to his car.

"Hello there. What was all that about?"

"He's still trying to persuade me to move in with him before Finals, so that we can see something of each other when I'm not revising," Alison answered.

"Are you going to?"

"I don't know. I like having my own room in College. I've got it just the way I like it now. Anyway I always read in bed until late and Oliver doesn't like the light on."

'A · year ago,' thought Charlotte, 'you would have considered early nights a small sacrifice for living with Oliver.' But she said nothing.

"What do you think I should do?" Alison was saying, wrestling with a plastic bag of books which kept slipping off the metal carrier. "And why do you keep looking up at the sky?"

"Debris," said Charlotte darkly.

Alison let that pass.

"Anyway don't ask me. I'm biased. If you move to Salisbury Street I'll be neighbourless."

"But it's only down the road." Alison straddled her bicycle and hung the bag from the handlebars. "I'll be back and forward all the time."

Charlotte was not convinced. It was the thought of Alison's instant availability that she found hard to relinquish. Sitting in Alison's creaking rocking-chair, lips stained with cheap red wine, the pale outline of the Bodleian beyond the window reminding them of the work they were not doing, had become an irreplaceable part of Charlotte's life.

Tyrone was interesting to talk to — at least he had been up until the accident. Patrick was intelligent and amusing enough, too. But they were men, and sometimes when she got into discussions with them, she felt as though they were talking to each other from the opposite sides of a great chasm, every other word getting lost on the wind.

"What's your ideal man like?" Patrick had asked her one day, hoping, Charlotte imagined, to hear a description of himself. She had pondered for a moment before saying, "My ideal man is a woman."

Back at College the odour of boiled vegetables was wafting into the street. The hot weather had brought all but the most committed out of the library and on to the front quad. Several people were stretched out on the grass asleep. Discarded books lay open and unread, their pages fluttering idly in the breeze. There was a message pinned to the notice board in the lodge. ALISON, CHARLOTTE. PUNT BOOKED FOR 1.30. PATRICK AND TYRONE. While Alison scanned the rest of the messages, Charlotte wandered into the street, attracted by a commotion in Radcliffe Square. A striking-looking woman in a red sports car was talking in heated tones with a traffic warden.

"You can't park here," the latter was saying. "Vehicles aren't allowed."

"Look here," the woman spluttered. "I've been driving around this bloody town for half an hour trying to find a parking space. I am just going into that building for two minutes," jerking her thumb in the direction of the college. Sighing, the traffic warden began to write out a ticket. The small crowd of onlookers gave a cheer as the driver jumped back in her car and jammed it into reverse with a horrible grating noise. Alison strolled up.

"Oh my God," Charlotte heard her say, as the car screamed to a halt beside them.

"Charlotte — this is my mother."

2

'...the fiendish crowd / Of shapes and thoughts that tortured me.'

Tyrone was trying to make sense of the hieroglyphics which he had scribbled in the margin of his Coleridge during the second half of the lecture. Already the arrows, underlinings and comments had begun to lose their significance, although he was sure that at the time of writing they had made perfect sense.

'My eyes make pictures when they are shut.'

Why had he underlined that? Oh yes. He thought he remembered. He looked closer. It was not an underlining after all, but a hair. He laughed, scattering cigarette ash on to the page, and brushed it away leaving a series of tiny grey streaks. He stubbed the cigarette out in the already brimming ashtray. The heat was making him feel drowsy. An enormous bluebottle, drugged and sleepy from the sun, suddenly stirred itself and started buzzing around his head. He flicked it away irritably, but it kept droning relentlessly round him making smaller and smaller circles.

'It's going to bore into my head in a minute,' he thought with a shudder, and leaping up, thrashed his arms at it ineffectually in the direction of the open window.

He felt incredibly tired. 'I mustn't go to sleep,' he thought. 'I must stay awake.' His latest series of nightmares had been so horrific that he awoke more drained and exhausted than if he had never slept. He had even tried taking naps in lectures instead of at night, because the soothing voice in the background tended to filter reassuringly into his dreams, whereas alone in the dark he was at the mercy of the demons of his imagination. He picked up the volume again and forced himself to look at it, but his head started nodding and the words sounded like meaningless chants.

> In Xanadu did Kubla Khan
> A stately pleasure-dome decree
> Dee-dum dee-dum dee-dum dee-dum
> Dee-dum dee-dum dee-dum dee-dum—

His head rested on the book and he surrendered.

He was clinging to a rock face. The wind was tearing through his hair, nearly pulling him off the ledge. Huge birds were flying around him, screeching and trying to claw at his face. He could not fight them off because he dared not let go. One hand was wedged into a crack so tightly that he could no longer feel it. And far below him a boy with sandy hair was sprawled over the stones. Now he was lying flat on a broad ledge, his hand running with blood, and he was crying, but the white birds were sitting on his chest, squashing the breath out of him, screaming and calling his name.

Tyrone sat up with a jerk. The yelling was coming from down on the pavement, not from inside his head. He staggered to the window, disorientated, and nearly fell out with dizziness. Charlotte was calling up at him. Something about a river. Of course. It was Patrick's birthday and they were going punting. He waved his assent and shut the window. 'Must get a ground-floor room,' he thought. 'Make a note of it now.' He scrabbled around for a pen but each one he tried expired after the first squiggle. He licked his finger. ROOM he wrote in the dust on his mirror, and then looked closer at his reflection. Tears and sweat had partly dissolved the page that he had been using as a pillow, and some of the print had come off on his cheek. He could just about read the world 'Ancient'. Washing his face with cold water he felt more alert. Then he opened the wardrobe and dragged out his mountaineering gear. Why had he kept it? he wondered. He would never use it again, ever. It was nothing but a merciless reminder, challenging his right to be alive, to read, to go to the river on a sunny day.

Bundling boots, crampons, ropes, pen-knife and ice-axe into a canvas bag, he carried it downstairs to where Charlotte and the others were waiting.

From a small black and white photograph on the mantelpiece, the sandy-haired boy stared into the empty room.

The same morning, Boris Gutkin was sitting at his kitchen table putting the finishing touches to a home-made birthday cake. Being blind, he had required some assistance from his wife, Ilsa, and was nursing a secret anxiety that a silver teaspoon, which seemed to be missing, had found its way into the mixture at some stage of the cooking process.

He skimmed his hand over the top of the cake, leaving a series of fingerprints in the icing sugar, and pressed a candle into what he estimated to be the centre.

In the background, an Esperanto tape of *Romeo and Juliet* was playing. That was Boris's little joke to annoy Patrick. The first time Patrick had heard it he had said patiently, "Boris, the language of Shakespeare is one of the most sublime sounds ever created. This sounds like a Spanish street brawl."

He had met his unlikely friend at an 'Introduction to Esperanto' meeting. Although Patrick had initially been quite interested in the subject, he was soon far more interested in Boris himself. In spite of being blind from birth, he had escaped from Poland to Britain in 1939, and had become a concert clarinettist. As Patrick played the flute, they occasionally scratched out a duet together, and no matter how much Patrick faltered and squeaked, Boris would become choked with emotion.

Ilsa, half-way up a ladder hanging wallpaper in the front room, saw Patrick approaching and waved.

"Happy Birthday," she called out, as he poked his head around the door.

"Hello, Ilsa. That's nice wallpaper," as she smoothed it with a fat brush.

"Yes, at first I couldn't decide—" she began.

"Yes," Boris interrupted, bustling in. "The important thing when choosing wallpaper—"

"Boris, don't be preposterous," she exclaimed.

Patrick laughed.

"If Beethoven could compose music, surely you will allow me the humble fantasy of choosing wallpaper," Boris replied good-humouredly, lighting a match. Patrick was always amused by the precise, measured way Boris spoke, as though every word was a literal translation. He lit the candle and Patrick blew it out dutifully before cutting three generous slices of cake. Patrick chose the one with a spoon handle sticking out, and surreptitiously removed it and placed it on the table.

"Patrick," Boris began in a conspiratorial voice, when Ilsa had left the room and could be heard clattering around next door, "I wonder if you could assist me with a semantic problem."

"Hm?"

"I was listening to a radio programme yesterday about photographic models, and much was made of the word 'cleavage'. Can you explain this term?"

Patrick considered. "Well, Boris, it's generally used to describe the . . . er . . . gap between a woman's boobs."

"Boobs, you say. Yes . . . very good." Boris was clearly impressed with the term.

"The cleavage is considered quite alluring." Patrick sometimes wondered whether Boris was having him on.

A shadow of a smile flickered across Boris's face. "But surely it is the, ah, boobs, themselves that are more alluring?"

Patrick had never before contemplated the subject with such a degree of abstraction. "I suppose it is the cleavage

15

which implies the presence of the boobs, and the imagination is often better than reality."

Conversations with Boris always had a very theoretical flavour. Even their recent trip to a local hamburger bar had assumed the properties of a philosophical enquiry. Boris, who had never before encountered fast food, was intoxicated at the thought of such dietary truancy, and even discarded his tie in an appropriate gesture of rebellion.

"I see you've abandoned your usual sartorial elegance," Patrick noted, steering him down the street.

"Yes," Boris smiled archly. "I thought a little informality was appropriate in the circumstances."

Patrick had guided Boris to a table in the corner as far away from a group of teenagers as possible, and sent the truculent waitress away three times while he tried to explain the menu. By the time Boris had decided on an inexplicably named 'International', the restaurant had started to fill up. Some young girls at the next table were smoking ostentatiously.

"Right. There's a fried egg at six o'clock, a beefburger at nine o'clock, and a sort of articulated sausage at eleven o'clock. Everywhere else it's chips and beans."

Unused to tackling food that had not been previously reduced to mouthful-sized pieces, Boris, without waiting for further instructions, speared the whole fried egg. Patrick watched in horror as it flapped and wobbled half-way to Boris's mouth before slithering off the fork and subsiding back on to the plate, sending chips skimming across the table. One of the girls opposite, whose dyed blonde hair was scraped into a frizzy clump just above her left ear, put down her milkshake and gave her neighbour a nudge. Patrick gave her a murderous glance. Mercifully Boris had moved on to the chips. Silently, Patrick reached across to his plate and tried to cut up the sausage. Boris skewered a newly liberated chunk, making Patrick withdraw his knife hastily. The blonde girl gave a snort.

"This is a most interesting experience," Boris was saying, when Patrick's knife slipped off the beefburger and clinked audibly against the side of the plate. He froze.

16

"Patrick, are you cutting up my food?" Boris demanded.

"No," he floundered, "I was just putting a chip back on to your plate." Patrick could see from his expression that he had humiliated the old man, and made a silent promise that he would never again be such a petty slave to embarrassment.

"Come into the Time Room," Boris was gesturing with his slice of cake, sending showers of crumbs flying. "I have something for you."

The Time Room was Boris's junkery, and was so called because of his peculiar arrangement of clocks. The room contained one grandfather clock, which told the correct time, and eleven other chiming clocks set five minutes in advance of one another. By recognising each distinctive chime, Boris never had to wait more than five minutes before knowing the time. For example, when the old wooden carriage clock over the fireplace went 'clunk clunk', it was twenty-past two, and when Mickey Mouse went 'ping', it was five-past one.

By a triumph of mismanagement, Boris also kept his piano in this room, and playing over the ticking became a battle of wills between Boris and his army of metronomes.

Another curiosity of the room was a grotesque rubber plant called Uncle Solly, which reared up in the corner, obscuring part of the window and keeping the room in permanent gloom. Patrick had thought the christening of the plant a pleasing eccentricity until he found out that it had been so named because Ilsa occasionally put a spoonful of her Uncle Solly's ashes in the pot.

Boris was sitting at the piano. "I composed this piece for your birthday. It's called 'Patrick's Song'," he said with some embarrassment, and launched into it before Patrick could speak. As the music filled the room, Patrick found to his consternation that he had a lump in his throat like a cricket ball and his eyes were watering. 'Thank goodness he can't see me,' he thought, pressing his knuckles against his eyes. He was usually scrupulous about extending the same

17

courtesies to Boris as he would to any sighted person; smiling, making eye-contact and looking interested even when he wasn't, just in case it turned out Boris had been bluffing all along. On this occasion though, Patrick took advantage of his own invisibility with some relief.

As the last notes were absorbed into the ticking, Boris turned round and beamed at him. Patrick groped for something to say, but everything that occurred to him was either a terrible cliché or simply inaccurate.

"Well, do you like it?" asked Boris finally, his face falling.

"Yes — very much. I'm sorry. I was just standing here listening to the music and thinking that anything I said to you about how good it was, or how much it moved me, would be a travesty of what I really felt. It would just be a quotation. Does that make sense?"

"Yes, of course." Boris stood up and walked over to the open window, listening for a second to the sound of the birds. "And consider how much more a blind person is the prisoner of language. The whole visual element of communication is removed. That is why I often prefer music to conversation. It is less mendacious . . . but this is precisely the problem I have been finding with my latest project — look," and he pointed to a desk on which were a strange-looking typewriter and a pile of what looked like blank papers.

"A Braille typewriter," said Patrick, fascinated.

"I'm writing my autobiography," Boris confessed, almost as if it was something that needed an apology. "I have been encountering exactly the problem you have just described." He stroked the top sheet thoughtfully. "You see, here I am trying to describe my mother, and how she appeared to me when I was young, and I want to show what an angel she seemed, but I can't do that without making her sound like everybody else's mother. How can I express this feeling without recourse, as you say, to quotation? Every word I write feels as though it has been plundered from other writers on the subject. And yet all I want to convey is that she was unique."

"It must be so much worse with autobiography," Patrick was thinking aloud.

"Yes," agreed Boris. "If I am not absolutely scrupulous in my choice of words, everything I write will be a misrepresentation of the truth. I am consequently making slow progress."

"How much have you written so far?"

"I have yet to complete my first page," Boris admitted.

"Well, that's still an improvement on my thesis," said Patrick, and they both laughed.

"Ilsa says I think about things too much," Boris went on as she came in, carrying three cups of coffee on a tray. "Don't you, my love?"

"She's probably right," said Patrick, smiling at her. Ilsa looked tired and overworked but, as ever, radiated kindness and warmth. As well as looking after Boris, with his continual whims, Ilsa worked as a nurse at the nearby hospice and so always had the air of someone putting a brave face on exhaustion.

"She's always right," cried Boris, flinging his arms round her and knocking the tray out of her hand. Patrick and Ilsa jumped back, yelping as the hot coffee splashed over their legs.

Boris, full of apologies, started dabbing at Patrick's dry leg with his hanky, while Ilsa fetched a cloth and rubbed soapy water into the carpet. Patrick decided it was time to leave. As he was going, a young man in a habit, with shaved blond hair and pebble glasses, was walking up the path. Boris insisted on introducing them.

"I'm so glad you've met. This is Greg. He belongs to the Brotherhood of Enlightenment whose meditation classes I attend. You must come along one evening, Patrick. This is Patrick, my good friend and ... er ... fellow Esperantist."

They shook hands politely, Greg holding on a moment longer than was necessary, and staring at Patrick with penetrating blue eyes. "I'm very pleased to have met you. I'm sure we'll meet again."

3

"SURELY the function of the Women's Movement should
be to campaign on major issues like abortion, contraception and equal opportunities, instead of worrying about
typhoons called Tracy, and renaming manholes."

Alison's mother, Vanessa, was dangling one foot over the
edge of the punt and gesturing with her cigarette. Alison had
reluctantly invited her along rather than miss the outing
herself. She was partly proud, partly suspicious, of Vanessa's
modern attitudes and her ability to ingratiate herself instantly
with people twenty years younger. Friends usually ended up
complimenting her on her mother, which always seemed the
wrong way round to Alison. After all, she could hardly be
congratulated for having been born. But it was inevitable.
Vanessa was so conspicuously enviable, with her invincible
confidence, her glamorous job on a women's magazine, her
expensive clothes, her independence. Alison was also
dismayed at the way her own personality seemed to shrink
to about a quarter its normal size in her mother's luminous
presence. She had made an unconvincing attempt at
exuberance and vivacity on the way to the river and had
since subsided into lethargic silence.

"It seems to me that language is the obvious place to start,"
Charlotte was saying, thrusting the punt pole forcefully
into the mud. "How are we supposed to communicate our

20

grievances if the language we have to use is already a weapon loaded against us."

"That's certainly an interesting angle," Patrick conceded.

"This is not an angle, Patrick," Charlotte corrected him. "This is looking at it head on. When I hear expressions like 'manpower', 'chairman', 'manhole', 'so-and-so mastered the situation', 'I now pronounce you man and wife', I honestly feel invisible. The other day I heard a documentary which used the phrase, 'The Fijians and their women . . .'"

"You should have written to the producer," said Vanessa, stubbing her cigarette out on the side of the boat.

"If I wrote a letter of complaint every time I came across an instance of sexism in the language, I would spend more time at my writing desk than the heroine of an eighteenth-century novel."

The dispute had arisen from one of those trivial incidents which gather momentum until everyone is dragged in. Alison had tripped over a protruding manhole cover on the way to the river and sworn at it.

"You mean 'Bloody access chamber'," Charlotte had corrected her.

"But everyone finds language inadequate," said Patrick, his mouth full of sandwich. "Only this morning I nearly offended someone because I wanted to pay him a compliment and the words I needed simply didn't exist."

"Yes, but women have to cope with its male bias as well as its insufficiency." It infuriated Charlotte that Patrick was unable to follow a rational argument without changing its direction, or making it anecdotal. "What I'm complaining about is our exclusion. Do you know there isn't a single word to describe a woman who enjoys sex, which isn't a term of abuse. Think of 'stud', 'casanova'. All we've got is 'nymphomaniac'. It is because of such omissions that my mother refuses to believe in their existence."

Vanessa gave a complacent smirk.

"No." Patrick had obviously been working it out. "I think it's the other way round. It's popular attitudes which form the language, not vice versa."

"Well anyway," Charlotte ploughed on, "it's a self-perpetuating system which serves the interests of men and leaves women with a voice which betrays us every time we speak."

'I wish I'd watched where I was going,' thought Alison. Unlike Charlotte, who saw arguments as a form of intellectual workout, a chance to flex her rhetorical muscle, Alison always ended up feeling tearful if she could not convert people. The atmosphere had been strained before they even started. She had had to walk ahead with Vanessa while Tyrone dropped his mountaineering gear into the river, to prevent her asking tactless questions.

"He went climbing in January with an old schoolfriend, Sean, and Sean was killed in a fall," she had whispered. "Tyrone sometimes gets these bouts of depression. We never mention it in case it upsets him."

Alison decided to take over the pole. She and Charlotte clutched each other as they changed places, making the boat wobble dangerously. The sunlight was pouring through the leaves, sprinkling the water with spoon-shaped shadows. Tyrone was throwing little pellets of bread to some ducks which were coasting beside them. He was continually called upon to parry collisions with the paddle, as they zig-zagged from bank to bank.

Alison could see her mother's shiny red hair rippling in the breeze, and the wisps of smoke drifting upwards. Water was pouring down her sleeve from the punt pole.

"The trouble with trying to change people's attitudes," Patrick was saying, "is that people have got out of the habit of thinking about issues, pursuing lines of thought to a conclusion. We are so used to having everything flashed up at us in unconnected gobbets — 'Vote Conservative', 'Give an Argy some Bargy'. I read an article the other day about some Soviet children who had contracted leukemia after a radiation leak, and the headline was '50 Red Tots Die'. Even art is being reduced to the simplest graphics. You don't need to vote for a political principle any more — you can vote for a red triangle or a blue square. It's all fast food, headlines, jingles, slogans. I'm surprised there isn't a telephone 'dial-a-summary' service. Some TV celebrity giving a five-second resumé of Plato's *Symposium* or the Special Theory of Relativity: 'Jewish Boffin in Twice the Speed of Light Shocker. Pip pip.' We're all being programmed not to think for ourselves, not to be able to concentrate for more than ten seconds at once."

"Ouch," said Tyrone, hastily withdrawing his foot, after one of the ducks had paddled over and nipped it.

"There's no hope for our generation then. We've already been programmed." This was Alison's first contribution. She always found she got half-way through a sentence and then forgot where it was going, and by the time she had remembered, someone had interrupted and the discussion had gone careering off down a new path. Perhaps Patrick's ten-second concentration span theory was right. "The only thing we can do, is bring up our children better than we were brought up." Her mother was very still. "Protect them from these moronising influences, and then they'll go one better with their children, and if each generation could wear away at a little ignorance and prejudice ..." she felt her train of thought slipping away ... "then society would be better than it is now," she finished feebly.

"Rubbish," said Vanessa belligerently. "There's no such thing as a universally better society. 'Better' means one that satisfies more of your own personal prejudices. I might think it was worse."

"No, you're wrong," Alison replied, driving the punt into the bank with a thud. "There must be a universal better. It has to be better to eliminate war and racism, and sexism and all the other isms. You can't tell me that's just a matter of my personal taste." She was getting breathless with frustration at not being able to express herself eloquently enough, knowing that this was a battle of rhetoric rather than principles.

"Well, I can't agree there," said Vanessa, as if that settled it. "No thank you, I won't have any birthday cake," she went on, waving away Patrick's offering. "I've just spent a small

23

fortune joining a new slimming club." She patted a non-existent stomach. The punt hit the opposite bank with a shudder.

"Do you think someone else should take over?" Vanessa asked, feeling the back of her neck cautiously. "Go on, Patrick, before she dislocates my spine."

"No, I'm fine," Alison said firmly, pushing off again.

"War is unfortunately the natural condition," said Tyrone seriously, massaging his big toe. "Ultimately we would all be prepared to kill in order to survive. Look at animals. Besides, it's the most effective way to keep the population down."

"Oh, I don't know," said Charlotte. "I've always rather favoured castration."

Vanessa let out a shriek of laughter. She was enjoying herself immensely.

'Why can't she just go home?' Alison thought miserably. 'Why does she always undermine me? Why can't she behave like normal mothers?'

Patrick was cupping his hands around Vanessa's cigarette as she tried to light it, their faces very close. Charlotte was lying back with her eyes shut. The sun was reflecting off Tyrone's dark glasses. Alison was unobserved. Thrusting the pole hard into the mud, she gave a cry and threw herself into the river. The icy water surged over her head, pouring what felt like gallons into her ears. She forced the air out of her lungs and struggled to stay under, waiting to see who, if anyone, would jump in after her. When those left in the boat heard the splash and saw the punt pole standing upright in the water they had found it enormously funny, but their laughter instantly changed to alarm as Alison did not re-emerge. Before Charlotte or Tyrone could scramble up, Patrick had flung himself inelegantly over the side, nearly capsizing them, and hauled a gasping Alison to the surface.

The other three, still too surprised to mobilise themselves, were drifting helplessly downstream broadside into the path of an oncoming canoe before Tyrone remembered he still had the paddle, and began propelling them slowly back to the bank.

Patrick, dragging Alison heroically from the freezing water, was feeling mildly elated at this opportunity to prove himself a man of action; he always had a sense with Charlotte and Alison that they regarded him as an honorary woman. This brought with it certain privileges, but it also had its drawbacks. Although he was happy to bask in the aura of political enlightenment, he was not so keen on the mantle of asexuality which it seemed to have conferred on him.

He had always been popular with women — 'as a friend' — he couldn't count the number of times that phrase had been used as a repulse. "I like you as a friend." It didn't seem possible that such innocent words could, given the right circumstances, become so loaded with sexual rejection. He had never been the aggressively heterosexual type who could not even say hello to a woman without giving the word half a dozen other connotations, and for this reason women felt at ease with him. But, and this was a constant source of bitterness to him, things rarely went any further. It riled him that for all their vocal support for the new androgyny, his female friends still seemed to be physically attracted to the traditional male. It sometimes appeared to Patrick that university was the best time of a woman's life precisely because it gave her the chance to live with women and sleep with brutes. Alison, for example. Not that Oliver was a *brute* exactly. And he couldn't blame Oliver for fancying her — he did himself. But he blamed her for submitting to the stereotype of the adoring disciple, and worse, he blamed himself for having failed to seize the same opportunity when it arose.

They had been at a party at a gothic-looking house set back from the Banbury Road. It was Hilary term of Patrick's final year and he had just split up with his girlfriend, Ellen. She was at the party with her new boyfriend, and although Patrick was not as disappointed as he had a right to be, he was worried that other people might interpret his indifference as smouldering jealousy.

It was a typical student party: the crowd was rather like salad dressing — no matter how vigorously it mixed, the component parts would inevitably separate and repel one another. There was one group in the back room smoking dope, another group jigging around half-heartedly to some music, and a third, of which Patrick was one, standing in the kitchen drinking and getting morose.

Alison was there too, and paying Patrick more attention than usual, her motives, he suspected, a mixture of pity and lack of other acquaintances to hand. When it became obvious that they were only talking to each other anyway, and the party itself was becoming intrusive rather than entertaining, Patrick offered to walk her back to College.

It was a warm night and they were both slightly drunk, giggling and stumbling into one another at the slightest excuse, and it would have been the most natural thing in the world for him to have pulled her towards him ... But his nerve failed him. When they reached her room and she invited him in, he felt his hopes surge again. He would read the situation carefully this time.

Her room was tidy, the bed was neatly made and there were flowers in a vase on the bookcase. A copy of *Twelfth Night* was open on the desk. It was a very feminine room — everything matched; nothing was left lying around that was not intended to be seen. It was paradoxical — Charlotte's room always had junk everywhere: clothes, old pill packets, bras dangling out of half-open drawers, records out of their sleeves, and yet he felt he could tell far more about Alison from what was *not* visible in her room.

She put on a record, then opened a packet of cigarettes. He did not usually smoke, and neither, he thought, did she, but he accepted anyway. There were a few inches of tequila in a bottle in the cupboard. They shared that too.

"I'm sorry about Ellen."

"Oh don't be. I'm not. I mean, I am of course. She's a really nice person. Was. Still is, I suppose," and in spite of himself he found he was talking about relationships, a subject he hated. But Alison was such a genuine listener, so unlike most people who never really listened at all but merely used the opportunity to rehearse their next speech, that he only realised how long he had stayed when they went to light up a cigarette and found they were down to the last two.

"My God, I didn't realise how late it was," Patrick apologised without moving.

The tequila bottle was empty. The record had finished and the needle was scratching away like a cat waiting to be let in. The conversation had ground to a halt. Alison stubbed her cigarette out slowly. There was a silence. They were dangerously relaxed. Alison went to stand up.

"Well . . ."

Patrick let the word roll around his mind for a few seconds, trying to work out what it meant. What it meant, at the very least, was 'this phase of the evening is now over. Something else is about to happen,' but he couldn't work out what. He was either being invited to leave or invited to stay, but she had made it deliberately ambiguous. The coward's way out would be to reply "Well?" and put the ball back in her court, but that was childish — it could go on all night like that. He stood up. She stood up, eyebrows raised.

Possible happiness, possible humiliation. Or dignity and disappointment.

"I must be going. I'm supposed to be getting up early tomorrow," and he had left, despising himself all the way home.

Alison, untangling a skein of green slime from one ankle, could hardly control her euphoria that it had been Patrick who had held her for that fraction of a second in their frantic underwater collision. It worried her that such a small event should make her feel so absurdly happy. It was just that she found it so difficult usually to think of Patrick as a physical entity. He seemed curiously disembodied, made up of some sexually neutral ectoplasm from neck to ankles. Besides, unlike Oliver, Patrick was definitely at the effeminate end of the male spectrum; slim, smooth skinned and sensitive. ('Pretty-boy' Weston, he had been known as at school to the

27

aggressive element — 'Spaghetti', to his friends.) In fact ever since that galling incident after the Banbury Road party, when she was *sure* she was giving the right signals, she had stopped thinking of him as heterosexual altogether. The discovery that beneath this veneer of genderlessness was a reckless spirit and a solid, male body seemed to Alison to have brought a new and potentially dangerous dimension to their friendship. She pushed the thought away. This was her usual practice with all time-consuming or disturbing ideas.

"What happened?" Charlotte asked when they were all sitting disconsolately on the bank.

"I just fell in and panicked," Alison lied with a shiver. "Sorry about your clothes, Patrick, and on your birthday too."

Patrick had removed his shirt and was wringing out a pair of muddy socks. Their jeans were plastered with mud and grass where they had scrambled up the bank.

"Poor you," said Vanessa brightly, patting her daughter on the shoulder. A hug would have been the ruin of a good silk blouse.

Tyrone did not say anything. Glancing at him, Alison was alarmed to see him staring at her with a strange expression on his face. 'He must have seen me jump,' she thought, hurriedly looking away.

Charlotte volunteered to rescue the pole and return the punt to the boat-house, while the others made their way back to the college. Vanessa decided to drive back to London. Tyrone caught up with Alison, who was already striding off towards the meadows. He squeezed her damp little hand.

"You shouldn't test your friends like that," he said. "Imagine the horror if none of us had come to your rescue. It would be better not to know."

4

VANESSA Laycott, Charlotte decided, was not at all like ordinary mothers. She had a good job and no husband for a start, which made her the antithesis of most mothers of Charlotte's acquaintance who seemed to have no jobs and lousy husbands. More incredible still, she made no comment on Alison's almost brittle slenderness, and no attempt to force-feed her with stodge. For Charlotte, a weekend back home meant running the gauntlet of fatty Lancashire hot-pot and great tombstones of fruit cake, her own mother believing that anyone under fourteen stone was flirting with anorexia.

Mrs Rowley was moderately short, moderately plump and moderately poor. In fact, her favourite fragment of received morality, 'Moderation in all things', ought to have been enough to drive any intelligent offspring to a life of debauchery and excess. She had never worked outside the home and tutted sadly at the thought of sixteen-year-olds coming home from school to an empty house. Charlotte was always exasperated by her continuous pretence of ignorance and inadequacy. "Yes. No. Ask your father," was the standard response to questions ranging in urgency from "Is there really a God?" to "Can I have more pocket money?" Charlotte remembered once asking her if she wanted anything to eat and watching in amazement as she turned to her husband and said, "Are we hungry, dear?"

Mrs Rowley's deference to her husband was, Charlotte soon

29

realised, purely notional. If she wanted to do a particular thing, she had an uncanny habit of planting the idea in his mind, and nurturing it until it finally matured one Sunday morning in the form of a muttered suggestion from the other side of the bed. Then she would marvel at the similarity of their thought patterns, and do what she had always intended, with the added security that if anything went wrong she could not be blamed for having suggested it.

Mr Rowley was the English Faculty librarian at the local university, a tall gangling man who was always searching for his spectacles. Although he kept the library immaculate, at home his curator's eccentricity burgeoned unchecked, and he managed to leave a continual wake of debris in every room. He was a pathological hoarder, and his trouser pockets, permanently stuffed with junk, bulged out sideways like jodhpurs. The filing cabinet in his study had long since ceased to function according to any recognisable system. Instead every drawer seemed to be labelled MISCELLANEOUS. Charlotte, fresh from her first-year literary theory course, told him it was because he was a latent structuralist, and thus had an innate distrust of the concept of alphabetisation.

"But I'm a librarian," he protested running a hand through his hair, leaving it sticking up in a great tuft.

Charlotte considered what Vanessa's flat in Kensington might look like in comparison to her own ramshackle origins. She imagined light, and space, and planning, rather than the haphazard assemblage of old furniture that her parents' relatives had foisted on them. The worn strip of carpet, tacked treacherously to the stairs; mock regency dining-room chairs with ugly wooden claws around the feet; and monstrous creaking wardrobes with stiff drawers which had to be jigged and rattled and finally kicked shut. The family car afforded Charlotte another instance of painful comparison with Vanessa's opulent lifestyle. Honky, the Rowleys' 1964 Morris Traveller, was the laughing-stock of the library car park. Charlotte could not recall a family holiday without instantly picturing the forlorn figure of her father, trudging up the hard shoulder into the distance to find an emergency telephone. Her mother, brother Rory and herself would be left behind to steam up the windows by drinking chicken soup, and play games of I-spy which never progressed beyond five turns: road, cars, grass, trees and sky.

Saturday afternoon invariably saw Mr Rowley prostrated on the drive, under the car, flinging out oily rags and expletives alternately. Finally, after wasting the entire day, he would swallow his pride and call the garage.

"Curse these maintenance manuals," he would say, pointing to a diagram of the engine, almost entirely obliterated by dirty fingerprints. "Never tell you anything useful like what to do when the last nut shears off."

"Or how to get engine oil off your best trousers," his wife would add pointedly.

The Rowleys inhabited a strange financial limbo, professing themselves rich enough to accommodate Charlotte's immoderate overdraft, but too poor to buy themselves a decent car, or furniture, or even any new clothes.

Though Mrs Rowley hated dress-making, she thought it was something she ought to do. Having little sartorial flair and a pessimistic image of her body, she tended to produce vast, tent-like floral ensembles, which she described as 'generous' and hid in the back of the wardrobe. The contrast with Vanessa Laycott's expensive elegance was dramatic. Charlotte could hardly recall a single evening of childhood television viewing unaccompanied by the clack of knitting needles, as her mother turned out another drooping cardigan for her husband to wear, fastened on the wrong buttons.

Every wall of the house seemed to be lined with books (mostly property of the library with a university stamp on the inside cover). Mr Rowley was no carpenter and had rigged up some shelving, using brackets and uneven planks secured in places with meccano. When she was young, Charlotte had surveyed the rows and rows of titles in amazement and incomprehension, imagining them to be part of some bizarre code. One that particularly fascinated and repelled her was a paperback, *Casebook of Critical Essays on 'The Rape of the Lock'*. It had a plain white cover with a picture of the spine

31

of a book on it. What could it possibly be about? she had wondered. A book about a book? She thought she knew what rape meant, and was fairly sure it had nothing to do with keyholes, or any other kind of lock she could think of. Another enigma was *The Cantos of Ezra Pound*, which sounded as if it ought to be an anagram. A dozen cups of thorn tea? What was this *Cantos* which belonged to the foreign-sounding gentleman, and who was the author?

Whenever she thought of her father, she always imagined him standing with his feet splayed out, swaying gently like a mast in a breeze, holding one of these books open at arm's length because he had lost his glasses.

Her mother, by contrast, she always imagined in motion, sprinting down the hall to answer the telephone, colliding with furniture like a large fleshy squash-ball, or running for a bus that was still half a mile down the road, with the rapid 'tock tock tock' of heel reinforcer on concrete. She remembered Vanessa's feline stroll and was filled with gloom.

Alison does not realise the advantages of a mother like Vanessa, Charlotte thought. Vanessa was after all more like a sister than a parent. They could swap clothes, go on holiday together, even go drinking together. Mrs Rowley refused to take her coat off in pubs in case someone spilt beer on it, and sat with her handbag grasped firmly on her knees, nursing a glass of orange juice. And both her parents were also far too polite to indulge in the aggressive routine of elbowing, shoving and waving money at the barman, but treated him rather like an auctioneer, trying to catch his eye from a distance. This tended to make an evening's drinking a thirsty and stressful affair, since by the time their semaphore had succeeded in securing a round of drinks, they were all too nervous and exhausted to go through the whole rigmarole again.

Vanessa no doubt was used to going out for business lunches and buying people drinks. In fact she was the sort of woman, Charlotte decided, who would have no qualms about going into a bar on her own for a drink. Her confidence in her right to do anything she pleased appealed to Charlotte.

Mrs Rowley was so used to putting herself fourth that she had long since ceased to identify any desires of her own which were not already dictated by those of others.

'Vanessa has broken a chain,' thought Charlotte, 'of generations of women, who deny themselves success in order to give their children a better chance, only to see their daughters postponing this gift for their own offspring. It's a spiral of self-sacrifice,' she thought, 'this perpetual deferral of fulfilment from mother to child, and it is going to stop at me.'

5

ALISON lay in the bath, her wet clothes gradually forming a pool of muddy water on the tiled floor. She put her head back and allowed her ears to fill with water. The eerie booming noise seemed to cut her off from the sounds and distractions outside herself. The splodgy pattern on the ceiling began to rearrange itself into recognisable shapes — the outline of South America; the craggy face of an old woman. 'Why can't Vanessa be like other people's mothers,' she was thinking. (Alison had for years called Vanessa by her Christian name at the latter's request.) 'And write me letters instead of turning up unannounced, and knit and worry, and make rhubarb crumble.' Alison had never recovered from the breezy tolerance with which Vanessa had countered her attempts at adolescent rebellion. She recalled joining a group of schoolmates who had turned vegan at the age of fourteen, purely to thwart, inconvenience and enrage their parents. Typically, she had had to suffer the ignominy of being the only one whose mother had decided it was an excellent idea, and replaced all their gourmet set meals with pumpkin seeds and mung beans.

Alison hauled herself out of the bath, sending a great wave on to the floor. The water had been far too hot and her legs and feet looked red and bloated. She dressed quickly, her dry clothes snagging horribly against her wet body. There was a ring of grey, foaming scum around the top of the bath.

She flicked water at it half-heartedly, squashed her puffy feet into tight shoes, and consigned her punting attire to a corner of the laundry.

On returning to her room, which in her haste she had forgotten to lock, Alison found a tramp sitting on her bed, rocking backwards and forwards and pulling stray threads from an already shaggy coat. He was completely drunk and stank like a public urinal. At first she felt like screaming and running, but realising that in his unsteady condition he hardly represented a physical threat, she began to calm down and tried to imagine what Patrick, or Charlotte, or even Tyrone, would do. She could not decide about Tyrone. His behaviour was so unpredictable. Patrick would have a friendly chat and then find him somewhere to stay. Charlotte would eject him vigorously and then write a letter to the paper deploring local housing provision. Oliver, she imagined, would eject him vigorously and write a letter to the local paper deploring tramps. Alison decided to give him a cup of tea and find out if he had anywhere to live.

"Goodness, it's hot in here," she said loudly, throwing the window open and taking a gasp of fresh air, while the tramp, tears leaking down his leathery face, slurped tea from a mug bearing the slogan FEED THE WORLD. She made a mental note to drop it in the bin later. He seemed to be spilling or at least dribbling more than he was swallowing, so gently removing the mug, she helped him up, saying, "Do you live anywhere?" which sounded silly, and "I'll take you home." He mumbled something inaudible but she eventually managed to coax him into telling her his address. Botley Road. Bracing herself, she began to propel him in the right direction.

Half-way down George Street, by which time he was leaning almost all his weight on her, overpowering her with the combined odours of alcohol, incontinence and rotting teeth, she was horrified to see the Dean, Mr Fairbrother, bearing down on her. Mistaking the tramp for a fellow student, he gave her a vague smile and hurried past.

The tramp was having difficulty walking. The soles of his

sandals, as if by a magnetic force, kept continual contact with the pavement, forcing him to shuffle along with bent legs. Every so often he would put on a spurt and stagger forward a few paces. Alison could not take her eyes off his feet. At first she had thought he was wearing dark brown wrinkled socks, but looking closer, she realised with disgust that what she was seeing was a combination of suntan, ingrained dirt and loose, ill-fitting skin. The filth was at its darkest and most intense around his toenails. She had a sudden vision of growing mustard and cress from the tips of his toes. 'Perhaps nausea is making me hallucinate,' she thought, coming to her senses just in time to stop him blundering into the path of a group of cyclists.

The house in Botley Road had flaking yellow paint on the woodwork, and filthy net curtains hanging up behind windows streaked and spattered with grime and paint. The garden had encroached almost to the front door, with weeds and grass reaching half-way up the ground-floor windows. A bicycle, horribly twisted and rusting, had been flung into the far corner of the garden, along with some planks of wood and pieces of mossy piping. A dismembered dustbin bag lay on the front step, spilling out egg-shells, soggy newspaper and a chicken carcase. A ginger cat shot through the hedge as they approached. A radio was playing in one of the upstairs rooms, its tinny chatter suddenly taking Alison back to her childhood and summer evenings on the balcony of her mother's Kensington flat.

Resolutely, Alison seized the knocker, which came away in her hand. She was trying to screw it back on when the door flew open and the landlord stood there, an unwelcoming scowl on his face.

"He's not coming back here," he said rudely, his cigarette wagging at her from the corner of his mouth.

"Why not?" said Alison politely, taking in her opponent's unsavoury appearance. He was standing with his arms folded intractably above his paunch, which was straining against his string vest like a basket ball in a fishnet bag.

"Because he hasn't paid last week's rent, that's why," he

replied, leaning one arm on the top of the door frame to reveal a sweaty clump of underarm hair.

"How much?" Alison decided that nothing would be too much to extricate herself.

"Thirty quid — and that's dirt cheap," he replied, jamming his hands in his pockets and staring expectantly at her handbag.

"How appropriate," she longed to retort, but instead handed over three ten-pound notes and the door knocker. The tramp, who had been moaning quietly and rocking to and fro throughout the exchange, seemed to revive and was hauled indoors.

"What's your name?" she called after him.

"Arthur Buck," said the landlord.

"Not you — him."

As the door slammed shut the tramp called out something indistinct like 'Harris'. It might at a stretch have been 'Magwitch'. 'Perhaps he's a millionaire recluse who will leave me all his money,' she thought, and then immediately felt terrible, as if her generous gesture had been nothing but a mercenary investment all along. She cursed her imagination for spoiling an act of kindness. Something Vanessa had said during the argument came back to her. "Look at you all — so young, so idealistic, so desperate to do the right thing." She had touched a nerve there.

When she got back to her room Alison found that Harris/ Magwitch had not only taken her camera, but worse, had urinated on the bed.

'A man from some far region sent / To give me human strength by apt admonishment,' she thought. Although Wordsworth's beggars never seemed to have such weak bladders.

It had seeped right through to the mattress, and the smell of him still lingered like a spectral presence. After a moment's consideration, she pulled a suitcase from the wardrobe and began stacking it with books, files, clothes and make-up. Parting with money was one thing, but mopping up bodily effluvia was quite another. She ran across the street to the phone box and called Oliver, who was half-way through a tutorial.

"It's me," she whispered.

"Oh yes," he said in his neutral 'I am not alone' voice.

"Guess what? I've decided to move in with you. Today."

"Oh good," he replied with guarded enthusiasm. "Well, I can't talk now. I'm teaching."

"See you later."

"Yes. Bye."

As Alison bounced along in the back of a taxi to Salisbury Street, it did not strike her as inauspicious that her sudden change of heart had not been dictated by love of Oliver, but by her fastidiousness about clean sheets.

6

PATRICK closed the lid of the piano and stretched. He was stiff from sitting hunched over the keyboard, trying to transcribe Boris's piece from memory. That was the trouble with Boris's compositions — they always proceeded straight from his head to the instrument, and like a druid's chants were never written down. He looked at the finished manuscript with its sprinkling of notes on staves like tadpoles in a net. The invisible had been made visible. He wondered whether to add any instructions as to interpretation. After all, now that it was released from the sanctuary of Boris's imagination and was there in black and white, it was, he thought, at the mercy of the musician. After some consideration he decided against it. Even if he filled the page with minute detail, no one could recreate the sound that he had heard in the Time Room on his birthday.

He did not normally try to write out Boris's compositions. In fact he found it an agonisingly slow business. However, he had been trying to tune into the news on the radio and had caught the last half of what was clearly a music competition. He had only picked up the fact that original compositions under three minutes long were acceptable, and that the first prize was one thousand pounds.

Something prevented him from mentioning it to Boris. He kept intending to tell him about the competition, but somehow the right occasion never arose. 'Anyway,' he thought, 'they would be glad of one thousand pounds if it was offered to them.' That made him feel better.

'Anyway,' he thought again. 'It won't win.'

Tyrone was sitting in his new room, reading the newspaper. The Bursar had been drafting a letter to a film company who wanted to do some night-shooting in the old quad, when Tyrone poked his head around the door. Dr Crow was also worried about the epidemic of obscene graffiti which was spreading like a disease around the college notice boards.

"Yes?" he said, beaming. Privately he suspected Tyrone of being one of the fraternity of nocturnal scribblers.

"I need to move into a ground-floor room ... I keep sleepwalking, and the other night I nearly fell out of the window."

"Oh dear." Dr Crow took off his spectacles and wiped away an imaginary smear. "How long has this been going on?"

Tyrone cleared his throat. "I've been sleeping badly since January ... since the accident. But it's only in the last few weeks that I've started actually sleepwalking. Probably the pressure of exams."

"Of course. How long now?"

"Five weeks," said Tyrone, panic gripping him.

"Well, we mustn't have you falling out of a window before Finals — I think there's a small basement room you can have." He opened a ledger on the desk and ran a fat finger down the page. "Yes, I thought so. This block, Room 3a."

Tyrone and Patrick had spent the morning shifting his belongings downstairs, and now he was sitting on his new bed reading the newspaper, and watching people's feet walk past the top of his window.

'I must get down to some work,' half of him was thinking, while the other half continued to scan the columns of print unenthusiastically. He was reaching the stage where there were only a few articles he had not read, and then he would be forced back to his desk. He slowed down, reading every

40

advertisement, job offer and obituary. His conscience had almost got the better of him when he saw it. There in the personal column, positively screaming at him.

> In Loving Memory of Sean, our
> only son, on what would have
> been his twenty-first birthday.

The words had sharp claws which leapt out of the page and sunk themselves into his eyeballs. Of course. Today would have been his twenty-first birthday. Should have been. A cloud passed over the sun, sending a dark shadow sweeping across the room. It suddenly seemed icy cold. 'I must get on,' he thought feverishly, snatching up his Shakespeare file from one of the boxes. Tragedies, Comedies, Problem Plays, Roman Plays. The folder was neatly sectioned off. 'How idiotic,' he thought, 'this way of slicing things up and naming them.' He imagined Shakespeare pacing up and down his cottage, ducking the tudor beams, announcing to Anne Hathaway, "I don't want any disturbances today. I'm writing my Roman plays."

He turned to the first page. Lists of quotations scooped up at random and flung down like confetti. The phrases seemed to cuff him round the head as he tried to learn them. He shut his eyes. 'Concentrate on the whole,' he told himself. 'Ideology.' But he could only think in fragments. He remembered Dr Beamish ringing the word 'ideology' in one of his essays and scrawling *Marxist clap-trap* in the margin. His mind was wandering now. He was very conscious of being inside his own body; of looking out through his eyes as though through a letter-box. Weird images swam towards him. Three witches chanting, a ghost rising up from the bottom of a cliff and filling the sky with its cries of revenge; Ophelia being hauled from the river, bloated and muddy. He pushed his knuckles into his eyes and a kaleidoscope of swirling red and black faces leered back at him.

Let me not be mad.

7

TWO weeks after her first encounter with the tramp, Alison knocked on the door of the Women's Refuge in Headington. Inside, Rosie Floyd, who was watering the plants from a saucepan, peered through the peep-hole. She had formerly relied solely on a door chain, until an incident a few months previously had persuaded her to take firmer precautions. A size eleven steel-capped boot had been jammed into the crack, splintering the door frame and snapping the chain as if it had been a lady's bracelet. In the ensuing scuffle, Rosie had received a broken nose, and the husband in question a suspended sentence. ("Extreme provocation . . . otherwise exemplary character . . ." the judge had said.) The final irony was that his wife had never even set foot in the refuge, but had run off to Cardiff with her aerobics instructor.

"What do you want?" crackled the white grille beside Alison, making her jump.

"I was wondering if you had a spare room," she replied, addressing the porch in general.

The door opened and Rosie swept her inside, slopping water on to the carpet. "You poor thing. Did he thump you, the bastard?" noticing a bruise on Alison's neck. "Have you got any luggage?"

"No, no," said Alison hastily. "It's not for me. It's for a friend of mine. I've probably come to the wrong place, but

I just don't know where else to go. I can't leave him where he is."

"Him?" Rosie stopped steering Alison into the kitchen.

"He's a tramp called Archie Harris, and he lives in this disgusting rented room. It's just a mattress on the floor, and there's damp, and mice."

Rosie pulled a face, but offered Alison a seat at the table and switched the kettle on.

"Most of the time he sleeps rough, but he's quite intelligent, and I thought if only he had somewhere warm and clean to live he might regain a little self-respect."

Rosie spooned powdered coffee into two mugs. "I'd love to help you, darling, but I can't have him in this house. I've got women here in such a state that they lock themselves in their bedrooms when the gas man comes to read the meter. They think it'll be their husbands in disguise. Sugar?"

Alison nodded gratefully. "I'm sorry to be wasting your time — I suppose I should just go to the council and try to have some action taken against his landlord. The house is so squalid. This isn't run by them, is it?"

The dark wooden furniture, trailing plants, and stained glass around the large dusty windows gave the place an air of seedy elegance, which Alison did not associate with institution decor.

Rosie was wrestling with a well-sealed packet of biscuits

"No, this was left to me, which was just as well or I would probably still be living with my brute of a husband. I'm a refugee too."

"Do you get a grant for running it?" Alison dunked her biscuit for a fraction of a second too long and it slumped to the bottom of the mug.

"No, unfortunately," said Rosie. "The women here on Social Security contribute a bit towards the bills, but if someone turns up on the doorstep with no cash I don't turn them away." She licked her finger and rubbed at a dirty mark on her shirt cuff. "Most people don't stay long. The depressing thing is, most of them end up back with their husbands."

"Perhaps the husbands realise how serious the problem is when their wives actually leave," Alison suggested.

"You'd be surprised what amnesiacs men are," sighed Rosie. "For a week or so everything's fine, and then it's business as usual. The sad thing is, that having left the hostel to go back home, the women are too ashamed to come back a second time. I really need a nice fat grant to do the job properly. There should be better security and a residential counsellor. It all needs re-decorating too. See how shabby it is." She pointed to a patch of wallpaper around the light-switch, which was torn and streaked with dirt and scratch marks from generations of hands clawing at it in the dark. "I have a social worker friend who pops in, but there's only me to do all the cleaning. It's not enough. Women who come here need to stay in relative comfort, long enough to realise that loneliness in safety is preferable to companionship with violence."

Alison nodded. "But how do you make enough to live on?"

"Not from this place. I teach part-time at the Poly. If I really wanted to make money I would rent it out to students."

"I think it's wonderful you do this instead," Alison broke in. "I always feel guilty about how little I do for other people. Being a student is so egocentric, in a lot of ways. That's why I wanted to do something for this tramp. I feel an obligation to him anyway because he stole my camera and then the next day returned it."

"That's not my idea of an obligation," said Rosie, "but I'll tell you what I'll do." She led Alison into the garden. It had a square pond in the middle, surrounded by red bricks and thyme bushes, a slightly overgrown lawn and some craggy apple trees. The fences were festooned with climbing plants and budding rose bushes which had not been cut back, but allowed to sprawl unrestrained. On the side of the house was an annexe in the same Cotswold stone as the main block.

"This is supposed to be a studio," said Rosie, turning a large rusty key and launching her right hip at the door, which shuddered open. "I'm intending to decorate it for use as an office." She flicked the light on to reveal a decent-sized room with a worn grey carpet, old-fashioned cream wallpaper with large clumps of painted roses, and a single bed with a semi-circular wooden headboard. There was a two-ring electric burner on the floor, and a model of the *Cutty Sark* in a bottle on a low chipboard coffee-table. At the far end, a narrow, gothic-arched window with lead diagonals made Alison think of a disused chapel. The table was where the altar should be and the ship was obviously the icon.

"It's nothing special," Rosie was saying, "but he could stay here for a few weeks until something better turns up. I've got an old paraffin heater in the garage which would warm the place up. Probably make him high as a kite too."

'It would give him something to drink, anyway,' thought Alison, but instead she said, "This is really kind of you. You can charge him rent, you know. He does get some sort of state benefit."

"We'll see. My main concern would be him coming in the house, but as this has its own entrance that shouldn't be a problem." She handed over the key. "It's ready when you are."

Alison thanked her and cycled back to Salisbury Street, glowing with a sense of accomplishment. It was the first time she had felt truly light-hearted since she had moved out of her college room. Life with Oliver was not turning out to be the utopia of mutual support and intimacy she had envisaged. For a start, he was obsessively, neurotically tidy, and her habit of leaving the breakfast dishes out until evening, and slinging her wet bath-towel over the banisters, drove him to paroxysms of silent fury. She was also dismayed to find that on her arrival he had dismissed Mrs Wing who came in two mornings a week to clean. It seemed as if the household duties automatically devolved upon her as resident female.

She had at first wondered whether the obscure corners of his house which she had not yet inspected would reveal any traces of his first wife, but she had found nothing. Not a single photograph, not a letter, not even a line of unfamiliar handwriting in an address book. He had even cut off the inside corners of various books, where there had clearly once been a dedication. It seemed paradoxical that having taken such trouble to erase her from his surroundings, he insisted on bringing her up so frequently in conversation. Rosalind became a sort of reference point for their relationship — a standard of unacceptable behaviour.

"Rosalind always used to reek of cigarette smoke." So Alison would perversely be tempted to have a sly puff at parties, followed by a liberal spray of perfume and a packet of chewing gum.

"That's just the sort of remark Rosalind used to make," on the rare occasions Alison said something smart at Oliver's expense.

"Where's my fountain pen / cheque book / other sock?" Oliver would demand regularly. It was not long before Alison began to suspect that "Where is . . .?" was really a synonym for "Go and get . . ." and started replying, "Where you left it!"

"You sounded just like Rosalind then," worked like a spell to send her scuttling off apologetically to look for the missing object.

Subtly, her routine began to change too. Back at College, she had been used to working all day in her room, with short breaks to see Charlotte or Tyrone. Occasionally she would take the afternoon off if Patrick called round, then see Oliver in the evening, and work again late into the night. Now she found herself falling in with his rhythm. Up early making breakfast while he showered, and working until three when she realised he would soon be home. Then she would panic, whisking around the house scooping dirty clothes off the floor, throwing apple cores and chocolate wrappers into the bin, scraping, washing and wiping. By listening for the click of the gate she could make sure she was still visibly at work when he walked in with his regular "God, I'm tired," and perfunctory squeeze.

Early nights became part of the routine. Oliver insisted that it made no difference to him if she kept the light on until the early hours, but the morning after would complain of a blinding headache. He also seemed, now that he had her under his roof, reluctant to allow her the same freedoms she had taken for granted when she had had a room of her own. One evening she told him she was going to meet Tyrone and Charlotte to discuss their Renaissance paper.

"Why didn't you tell me before?" he asked, looking hurt.

"Because Charlotte only rang up this morning."

"Oh. Well, what am I supposed to do?"

"Do? Do whatever you like. Do whatever it is you expect me to do when you go out for your college dinners and sherry parties." It exasperated her that an apparently highly intelligent person was reduced to petulant insecurity at the thought of amusing himself for one evening.

Defeated, he changed tack. "What time do you want me to pick you up?"

"I don't — I'm cycling."

"But it's not safe after dark. I'd much rather pick you up. You just want me to sit here worrying."

"Oh, stop being so bloody parental," she half laughed. But she knew she would have to let him collect her just to keep the peace. She was always compromising nowadays. Even over trivial things like wearing make-up.

"You look beautiful when you wear make-up," Oliver said one day. Barbed compliments were his speciality.

"Meaning, I suppose, that I look hideous without it," Alison replied stonily.

"No, no, I didn't say that. Anyway, I always make myself look decent for you. I wash, and . . . and shave." There was an edge to his voice.

"I resent the idea that a woman isn't decent unless her face is painted," she said. "Washing just isn't comparable." At least she didn't actually say that, she merely thought it, along with other things like 'If I can't wear my real face in the presence of someone who professes to love me, who can I show it to?' She often did this, continuing the argument in her head, and winning it, whilst outwardly sitting in a sullen and defeated silence. It was the next best thing to assertiveness, she supposed. The next day, however, saw her

47

plastering on maroon lipstick and bright turquoise eyeshadow, thinking that if she looked sufficiently vulgar Oliver would insist she take it off. She had applied foundation with an orange tint that clashed brutally with the lipstick and left a deliberate tide-mark around her chin. They were going out to dinner with some old friends of his whom she had never met. Unluckily, Oliver, rather than finding her unpalatably gaudy, was delighted that his comments of the evening before had paid off, and hustled her into the taxi before she could protest. She hardly said a word throughout the meal, but sat there, writhing with mortification, and trying not to leave smears of Rollicking Ruby on the crystal.

Alison remembered the badges they had worn during the first-year rent strike. NO COMPROMISE above a little fist. She sometimes wondered if she should dig it out and wear it in self-parody.

Instead of turning in on himself, Oliver merely abused the piano in moments of frustration, pounding away, his foot jammed down on the loud pedal, making the plants on the top quiver and dance. He took his anger out either on the piano or the dog. When she came home late one evening she found him sitting in an armchair, changing TV channels with the remote controls. Beckford was lying at his feet with a dog biscuit inches from his nose. He had obviously been in that position for some time as he was whimpering quietly. Each time he made a move towards the biscuit, Oliver would raise his hand and boom, "*Stay!*" so that he cowered back again.

"That's cruel," Alison protested. "Go on," she urged the dog, but he still crouched there, pressing his body against the floor, gazing mournfully at the biscuit until Oliver said, "Go!" At this command, he seized it and slunk out of the room.

"It's just obedience training," Oliver explained. "They're much happier that way."

'That's what people said about slavery,' Alison thought. Another development that irked her was his change in attitude towards her academic ambitions. In the early days, when their relationship had taken the form of admiring disciple and indulgent pedagogue, he had been happy to praise and encourage her. Together they would get excited about an idea in one of her essays which illuminated a particular work in a new and bizarre way. Now that they were living in close proximity and Alison's days as an undergraduate were hastening to an end, she found him increasingly indifferent to her scholastic discoveries. Occasionally when she mentioned doing post-graduate work on the Romantic period, his own field, he would become very uncomfortable and issue dire warnings about its short-comings.

"Don't do it, Alison," he would say, as though she were considering a career in prostitution or drug-trafficking. "It's not for you. It's three years of poverty, slavery and disillusionment working for a doctorate, and it doesn't even guarantee you a job."

"You managed it." There was more than a hint of competitiveness in their relationship.

"That was some years ago now." He referred to the age gap in these imprecise terms. "I was lucky to have thesis material that was commercial enough for publication," he went on magnanimously. (Personally, he felt that talent had had the edge over luck, but did not feel that this was the proper time to suggest it.) "Besides, you wouldn't be earning any money for years — and we'd never be able to afford children."

'Children?' thought Alison, with mounting distress. She imagined a great pink, wrinkly growth invading her body, sapping her strength and making her inflate like a Zeppelin. She saw herself standing in supermarket queues with her legs apart, hands pressed into the small of her back, wincing with pain. Then there would be ante-natal classes full of other rotund vessels discussing swollen ankles and episiotomy. Then, finally, the slimy chrysalis ripping its way out leaving her permanently frigid, incontinent, and with an abdomen puckered like a pappadom. She squirmed inwardly. The idea of children appealed, in theory, from the age of about six when they would with any luck be attractive, intelligent and full of charming precocity. It was the filthy materiality of babies that appalled her. Was it any coincidence, she wondered, that babies only rhymed with other unpleasant words. Scabies. Rabies.

The future with Oliver was murky and indistinct. She did not envisage life without him, but at the same time could not fit him into any appealing scenario of how she would like things to proceed. The mention of children brought her once again to this impasse, and so she did what she always did on these occasions — ejected the thought from her mind and concentrated on the present. The present consisted of studying for Finals, keeping Oliver in a good mood, rebuilding Archie Harris in her own image, and hoping that the future would fall into place like a row of well-positioned dominoes.

8

THE silence in the room was so audible Patrick felt he could almost hear the dust particles colliding. The walls were plain white and the floor, on which he had been sitting cross-legged for half an hour now, was of varnished wood, and very hard. On a shelf at the end was a vase of dried flowers, but apart from that the room was quite bare.

He stared into Greg's eyes, only a couple of feet away from him, trying not to blink or twitch, and Greg's eyes, like a couple of brilliant blue marbles, stared back without movement or expression. Like a corpse, Patrick thought. His head felt heavy and unstable, as if his neck was as flimsy as a reed. He was beginning to wish that he had not allowed Boris to talk him into this visit to the Brotherhood headquarters. The stillness of thirty people meditating was beginning to oppress him. He was also terrified that he might at any moment break wind, an imminent possiblity given the quantity of bean and lentil bake he had consumed at the Brothers' restaurant earlier that evening.

Boris, typically, had implicated Patrick in the evening's proceedings, then cried off, leaving him to sit by himself and be served by Greg who was on duty until nine. Moreover he had not realised that meditation was going to involve sitting very close to Greg and maintaining eye-contact for over half an hour. Patrick found it difficult enough to look Boris straight in the eye — and he was blind. Besides he was not quite at ease with Greg. 'There's definitely something peculiar about him,' he had thought, watching as Greg showed some new arrivals to their table, without a flicker of emotion on his pale, angular face.

"Sit opposite your partner, cross-legged, with your arms resting loosely on your knees. Concentrate on their eyes, and try to empty your mind completely," the Brother at the front had said. "Forget yourself. Free your mind from its awareness of the body."

Patrick clenched his buttocks. He had never been so aware of his body in his life. Jeans were clearly the wrong thing to wear. They were cutting off the circulation at the knee. Most people were wearing loose jogging suits. A few of the Brothers were wearing robes. He kept being assailed by the urge to do something stupid, like yell out, or leap up and do a streak across the room. 'This is the most unrelaxed I have ever been,' he said to himself. 'Empty your mind. Empty your mind,' as if repeating the words was the only way of beating back a host of thoughts and images to the edge of his consciousness. The problem was, as soon as he stopped chanting to himself, they crowded back again to repossess him. There was the one about his doctorate. Was French puppet theatre something he really wanted to dedicate himself to for the next two years at least? If he gave that up what else could he do? It was a year since he had graduated, and he still had not managed to put anything down on paper. This led on to another memory — bursting into Tyrone's room one day to find him talking into a small hand-held device.

"I didn't know you used a dictaphone," he had said with interest.

"I don't. I use my finger," replied Tyrone. "Oh, you mean this. This is the solution to writer's block."

"And writer's cramp too, presumably."

"Yes. Lately I've been dictating my essays on to it, then typing them out. It bridges that abyss between the mind and the page."

"I didn't realise you found it so difficult. I thought it was because you always wrote so furiously that your handwriting is unreadable."

"No, actually. Mrs Summers is under the mistaken impression that I do not hand essays in because I am lazy or mentally unbalanced, or something. I'm probably both, but that isn't the reason. My mind literally races with ideas the whole time, but as soon as I start to put them down on a blank sheet of paper, I freeze up. I find I can't control the way the written words read — without my voice the black squiggles lose all their authority and become subversive and ambiguous. In fact I've noticed that the essays I read aloud always do much better than the ones I hand in."

He took the dictaphone from Tyrone and looked it over approvingly. "It's like having your own portable Boswell." He rewound the tape and played it back. It spluttered into life.

"It is no coincidence that Prometheus, the hero of Shelley's poem, also occurs in the subtitle of *Frankenstein*. His act of transgression in stealing fire from Jupiter is analogous to the Romantic view of the poetic imagination as an unhallowed appropriation of divine creativity. Coleridge's Ancient Mariner is the poet's *alter ego* — the killing of the albatross a symbol of the poet's own trespass into forbidden imaginative realms."

Then another memory. Seeing Tyrone dressed in a suit, and saying, "What are you all dressed up for? Got an interview?" and Tyrone saying,

"No, a funeral."

This brought back the punting trip, and rescuing Alison from the river, and his ridiculous sense of panic that she might die without ever having known that he loved her. It was perverse, but one of his most valued memories was a furious argument he had once had with her and Charlotte. Apart from the party, this was the closest to intimacy they had ever been. It had been over a film. Patrick and some friends were talking in the bar about going to see a cult horror film.

"You're not," Alison said in disbelief.

"Yes. Why not?"

"Because it's full of gratuitous violence and the victims are always young women. It's repulsive."

"But just because you go to see a film about violence doesn't mean you condone it," Patrick explained patiently.

"Of course it does," interrupted Charlotte, bristling. "You pay your money to the film-makers so they can make more of the same, and it promotes an entire culture that finds the mutilation of women entertaining."

"It's sick," Alison said, her forehead crumpled with disgust. The jukebox burst into song, drowning her words.

"But you're advocating censorship," Patrick protested, horrified.

"Too bloody right I am," Charlotte yelled back. "You talk as if it doesn't already exist. That junk is the most censored stuff around — all the objections of women like us have been censored out of it."

People in the bar were beginning to take an interest.

"Look, don't get so hysterical. Watching *The Butcher* is not going to make me go around cutting up women."

"It's not you we're worried about," said Alison. "It's the random lunatic in the back row."

"But lunatics will be lunatics whatever they watch," he said through a mouthful of crisps. "Who are you to tell people what is fit or unfit for public consumption? That's a basic denial of liberty," he crunched.

"What about my liberty to walk around after dark unmolested? I suppose that's a small price to pay so that you can go to the bloody movies." Charlotte was in combative mood. Alison was merely unhappy.

"You're over-reacting," he said calmly. This was dangerous. Charlotte was quite capable of replying, "Yes, that's right, I'm a hysterical woman who cannot be held responsible for her irrational behaviour," and tipping a pint of beer over his head. Instead, she and Alison rolled their eyes and exchanged a conspiratorial look of pity for the futile blusterings of men, which made Patrick shrivel.

"It's only a film," he finished feebly.

54

"Only a film?" Charlotte echoed in astonishment. "What do you mean only a film? Are you trying to tell me that fiction has no influence? I mean, you can't have it both ways. You cannot on the one hand say that fiction is an important social influence and therefore the state must fund my study of French literature, and then on the other hand say that films have no effect." Sensing victory, she was in full swing now. "If you really believe that, I suggest you give up your research into French puppet theatre and concentrate on something practical like growing turnips." And she sat back, satisfied that another moral dilemma had been neatly anatomised.

Alison's eyes were brimming. "Just being clever isn't the point, Charlotte," she said wearily. "What hope is there if the men we like and think we can trust have to have it all explained . . ." and she had pushed her way out, elbowing past people, one hand over her eyes. Patrick had not gone, of course. With the ingenuity of the desperate, he had concluded that her anger was an indication that she must care for him a little; his actions mattered to her. On reflection, though, it occurred to him that it was a dubious privilege to have gained someone's affection only to the extent that one now had the power to disappoint them.

Greg blinked for the first time, bringing Patrick back to the present. 'I wonder if he can tell I haven't been concentrating. Perhaps my pupils were dilating.' He became slowly aware that his lower legs were completely dead. 'I'm going to have to move them,' he thought anxiously, worrying whether it was dangerous to make sudden movements while people were meditating, rather like waking a sleepwalker.

Mercifully the man at the front rose, signifying the end of the session. Patrick stretched his legs out, enjoying the exquisite agony of pins and needles. It was one of those sensations where the relief more than compensated for the discomfort. Greg smiled as he watched Patrick massaging his feet.

"I could see you weren't really relaxed," he said.

"I must admit I didn't enjoy it too much," Patrick confessed.

"Enjoyment isn't the object, but you must come again. Like everything else, it improves with practice. Tea?"

Greg showed him into a side room which was also bright and bare, apart from more dried flowers and a few cushions which felt as soft and yielding as giant marshmallows after forty minutes of hard floor. He reappeared, carrying two cups of herbal tea. It tasted horribly bitter and seemed to leave a coating of fur on Patrick's tongue.

"I must say, I can't see Boris doing all that," laughed Patrick.

"He doesn't, to be honest. He only comes along to observe."

"But he's blind."

"I think that's rather appropriate, don't you? After all there's not much to look at in a meditation class. He mainly comes for a chat afterwards. When I first met him I hoped he would join us, but then I met Ilsa and realised it wouldn't be fair, so Boris is more of a social associate. We only encourage single men now."

"What does the Brotherhood believe in then?" asked Patrick, hoping to pre-empt any potential recruitment drive.

"It's not so much a matter of belief as of lifestyle. We believe in a certain lifestyle. For example, doesn't it strike you as monstrous that people take more care of their cars than of their own bodies?"

An image of his bicycle rusting quietly in the back garden rose up before Patrick unbidden, but he understood what Greg meant. "Yes, I suppose so, but however well you look after yourself, you are still at the mercy of hundreds of arbitrary disasters."

"That's right," agreed Greg, "so why compound the problem with complications of your own making — drugs, alcohol, cigarettes, promiscuity, stress, etcetera. That's our argument."

It was watertight so far, thought Patrick, but the cracks would soon show.

"We try to simplify things," Greg went on. "Think of the way most people live. They throw a couple of fish fingers under the grill, then while they're cooking, put some laundry into the washing machine, dash into the other room to catch the news headlines, then smell burning and rush back to rescue the fish fingers. Why live like that? We try to do just one thing at a time, and concentrate on that one thing so we can experience it to the full. If I'm chopping an onion, I think about chopping an onion, not about something I heard on the radio, or what I'm going to wear tomorrow."

Patrick was interested. "That all sounds sensible enough, but you don't need to live in a commune to do it."

"You do." Greg drained his cup. "If you try to undergo a complete change of lifestyle but still live amongst the same people, you are under constant siege to revert to your old habits. Besides, the Brotherhood is self-sufficient. We grow vegetables, and run the restaurant and meditation classes, so none of us needs to work outside the community. That eliminates the stress of ambition and the perpetual desire to accumulate possessions."

"But without ambition, how can you ever have fulfilment?"

Greg was ready with an answer. "It's all a question of changing your ideas about what constitutes fulfilment. Society's concept of success is so phoney — it always embraces notions of power, wealth and fame, so failure is built into the system. We would suggest that fulfilment comes from the very opposite of those things, from the renunciation of material wealth, and from anonymity. Egotism is the great evil. It is only surrendering the impulse to assert oneself all the time that brings true enlightenment."

"It sounds suspiciously like Christianity to me; the meek inheriting the earth."

"In a sense it is the very opposite of modern Christianity, which hinges entirely on faith. We try to concentrate on lifestyle — belief in any particular system is supplementary, in my view. I happen to believe in reincarnation among other things, but that's unimportant."

"But surely," Patrick was getting confused, "in order to reach this state of enlightenment, you have to become a sort of non-person."

"That's the idea, yes. Of course I'm nowhere near that state of neutrality. I am still a slave to my personality, but I'm working on it." He looked modestly down at his robe.

"Do you always go around in that gear?"

"Generally yes, unless I have to go into town for something — then I would wear jeans."

Patrick looked at Greg thoughtfully. One thing was particularly noticeable. He had no irritating habits, like fidgeting or nail-biting. Patrick became actutely aware that he had been twiddling his shoelace, and stopped. Greg sat opposite him as composed and inscrutable as the Sphinx.

"Why is it men only?"

"For the same reason that other religious orders choose to be single sex. It removes an entire dimension of stress — the element of sexual competition. Don't you sense it yourself, in mixed company, that undercurrent of aggressive preening and display."

"Ye-e-es," said Patrick cautiously, a vision of baboons baring their buttocks at each other suddenly coming into his head.

"That's what we are avoiding. You see, so often the sexual urge is nothing but egotism in its purest form. Conquest. Our founder, Brother Huw, always encouraged a more diffuse kind of love." He stopped, distracted by the sound of heavy rain bouncing off the roof. "Let's go for a walk," he said.

"It's raining, isn't it?" Patrick said politely.

"Yes. It's good to walk in the rain. Especially at night when the streets are empty. I hate to see people hunched under umbrellas. What's so terrible about getting wet?" He was hitching his robe above his ankles. "Come on."

It had obviously been raining for some time. They splashed along St Giles, through the shimmering pools of light from the street lamps above. Someone cycled past wearing a sou'wester and a fluorescent yellow cape which enveloped the bicycle. He was grimacing and twisting his face away from the rain.

"Look at that," Greg shook his head. "At our retreat in Wales where we take new recruits, the cottage backs on to some woods. We get fantastic mists in autumn, and those white, watery sunsets. Last October I was there for six weeks with this chap Lindsay, and I used to drag him out for walks in the rain at night. We'd come home plastered with dead leaves. He thought it was some sort of induction ceremony."

"You must have terrified the neighbours . . ." They smiled at each other.

"Luckily the village is about half a mile away. It's a perfect setting for people who want to join the Brotherhood. They stay there for two months with another Brother. No TV, no radio, nothing. Just talking, walking, gardening, meditating. We find those who last the full two months usually become Brothers. Most drop out after the first few days saying they're bored."

"It's worrying how dependent people have become on ready-made entertainment," Patrick was thinking aloud. "Some people would be driven out of their minds by one week of their own company. I suppose that's why TV is so addictive. It's a way of warding off a terrifying encounter with oneself."

"Yes," said Greg earnestly. They were cutting through the graveyard to the Banbury Road. "There's something almost tribal about the way we insist on marking out territories everywhere, too. This guy Lindsay got quite annoyed when I lay down on 'his' mattress one night, instead of the one I usually slept on. He couldn't handle the uncertainty of not knowing exactly where he was going to sleep each night. Then I noticed he always sat in the same place in the living room. So I moved the cushions. Just little things, like always using the same mug, as though it had some totemic significance, began to irk me. He was quite taken aback when I explained that this attachment to material things was precisely what we were trying to erode. He had already started saying 'my mug', 'my bed', 'my robe' . . . he left soon after that."

A young woman turned into the graveyard, and started as she saw Greg's pale habit against the graves. She put her head down and scuttled past without looking up, her wet hair glued to her coat collar.

Patrick could feel cold water running down his back. His socks squelched with every step. The rain was coming down even harder now as they headed up the Banbury Road. It was swirling along the gutters and gurgling in the drains. He wiped his fringe out of his eyes.

"Isn't this great?" said Greg, turning to Patrick. His face was shining with water, its pallor illuminated briefly by the headlights of a passing car. He had removed his pebble glasses and was straining his eyes with a look of intense concentration. It gave him the air of a martyr on a stained-glass window radiating some inner strength, thought Patrick.

"Yes," he replied, "bloody marvellous!" as a bus appeared out of the torrent like a mirage. The faces of the passengers were an indistinct blur behind the steamed-up windows, as it shuddered noisily past, spraying them with filthy water in a kind of muddy baptism.

9

THERE were now only three weeks left until the exams
and it was almost impossible to find a seat in the library
after nine in the morning. Alison seemed to have gone to
ground completely; Charlotte had not seen or heard from her
for days. Tyrone had become a creature of the night, living
in his own peculiar time zone; working through the hours
of darkness, sleeping during the day, drinking heavily, and
emerging at dinner, bleary-eyed and unshaven. Charlotte had
spent the previous day in the library, reading until it closed
at ten. Her brain felt like the victim of intellectual force-
feeding. It was as if someone had stuffed two straws up her
nose and pumped in the last eight volumes of *Critical
Quarterly*. She glanced in the mirror to check that she had
not become hydrocephalic overnight. A pair of bloodshot
eyes stared back at her. She stuck her tongue out. It looked
pale green and furry. Then she tried to pull the most
grotesque face possible. A hideous gargoyle leered out of the
mirror. She removed her fingers from her mouth and nostrils
and tried another face, wondering whether it was possible
to embarrass oneself in the privacy of one's room, or whether
embarrassment was dependent on witnesses. However stupid
she looked she could not raise so much as a blush. That was
not quite true though, she thought. When she re-read some
of her old diaries, quite alone, she found herself cringing in
every muscle. It was like eavesdropping on the thoughts of

a stranger, looking through those old confessions — as if her life was not a continuum but a sort of trade-up policy, where every five years or so she found she had been replaced without realising it by a new person. She felt eternally divided from the seven-year-old who had been afraid of the dark, refused to eat vegetables, and got car sick on long journeys. Or the twelve-year-old self who wanted to be an air-hostess, and went horse-riding, and could beat all the boys in her class at arm-wrestling.

She wondered how the next few years would change her. Not too much, she hoped. She thought she was pretty good as she was.

There was a knock at the door. She leapt away from the mirror as Tyrone tried to push his way in through the piles of books, clothes and records which were blocking the doorway.

"You're awake!" she said in amazement. "Don't you realise it's day-time?"

"I've got to get away from here. My car is outside on a double yellow line. Do you want to come to Hampton Court for the day? No books allowed."

If the Vice-Chancellor had walked in at that moment offering her an honorary degree and a one-way ticket to Barbados he could not have been more welcome than Tyrone and his rusty Avenger.

An hour later they were clanking down the slow lane of the motorway, a couple of bottles of beer and some chicken sandwiches gently warming on the back seat. It was a glorious day. The sky was cloudless; a filmy blue. Visibility was perfect. The countryside around was a fresh new green, fading gradually to a pale violet at the horizon. Charlotte could pick up even minute detail on houses several fields away. Tyrone had his window open, one arm resting on the ledge. Charlotte was pleased to see him looking so relaxed. Perhaps at last he was beginning to recover from Sean's death. For the last five months she had witnessed his passage through hysteria, depression and indifference. Charlotte had no experience of bereavement; she did not know anyone who had died. Her Uncle John had cancer, but all the time he was still alive there was the chance of a miracle. Consequently, she felt ill-qualified to distinguish between normal and excessive reactions. Generally, Tyrone had been reluctant to acknowledge that anything had happened, and with some relief and a little guilt, she, Patrick and Alison had gone along with this and avoided all allusion to the accident.

She stuck her head out of the window until her eyes ran. She felt as though the dust of ancient volumes, which she had been inhaling for the past three years, was blowing away down the road.

The noise of the engine made conversation a strain. The inside of the Avenger had the distinctive smell of old car — a combination of petrol, oily rags and plastic seat covers. Charlotte made an attempt at folding the map, before giving up and stuffing it in the glove compartment.

"I know we are supposed to be having a day off from books, but if you don't read the map we are going to get lost as soon as we come off the motorway," Tyrone shouted over the roar of the engine.

Charlotte wrinkled her nose. "I can't read maps. I can't even fold them properly."

In spite of this disclaimer, she navigated them safely around London. Tyrone stopped at a garage to fill up with petrol and came back with a packet of old-fashioned humbugs.

"Just like being a kid again," said Charlotte, helping herself. She noticed he was eating sweets today rather than smoking.

"I didn't realise it was visible from the road," he said, as they drove past Hampton Court. Charlotte too had not been there since she was a child and had forgotten how awesome it looked from the front. It was as large, red and imposing as Henry VIII himself after a few jugs of wine and a game of real tennis.

They strolled around the state apartments, which smelled strongly of old fabric and furniture polish. An American tour party was ahead and occasionally the voice of the guide floated through to them. "Jane Seymour died here in 1537 after the birth of the long-awaited male heir, Edward VI."

"What do you think of these places?" whispered Tyrone as they finally emerged into the bright sunlight.

Charlotte put her head on one side. "Part of me feels disgusted that so much money was squandered on a few privileged people," she spoke slowly and thoughtfully, "and the rest of me feels glad that it was, so that people like us can now have a share in them. I don't know which argument has the edge."

"Don't you feel jealous and frustrated that you will never have anything like it for yourself? Don't you want to own every last brick?"

"No, I don't think so. It's like Chartres Cathedral, or St Peter's. I don't want them for myself. I just want to be able to look at them. In fact, when I look at those enormous arches and pillars and the detail on every carving, I feel ashamed to be agnostic. Unfortunately the feeling never outlasts the visit."

"But a cathedral is different from a palace anyway. The motives for building them are at opposite ends of the spectrum. Have you been to Versailles?"

She shook her head.

"You must. You can't begin to imagine the sheer decadence of the place. It is so large that you can't actually frame it all in one glance — you have to keep turning your head to fit it all in. I first saw it when I was nineteen — I'd done all that French Revolution stuff in History. Standing in the forecourt underneath the statue of Louis XIV I was suddenly filled with these feelings of rage and aggression as if I was one of the peasants storming into Marie Antoinette's bedroom with my cudgel. But at the same time, everyone there including me was walking around like zombies with our mouths open, as if we were in church, because it was so fabulous."

"Let's go into the maze," said Charlotte who had been discreetly following the signs. She grabbed his arm. "I'll give you a twenty second start and still beat you to the centre."

Fortunately there were few people around. A school party was just emerging, eleven-year-old boys jostling and shoving each other into the bushes. They were followed at a cautious distance by an elderly couple, shaking their heads disapprovingly.

"Go on." Charlotte gave him a push.

"What happens if I get lost? I could be blundering around in here for ever. Aren't you supposed to unravel one of your stockings and leave a thread?"

"Not wearing any," she replied, as he disappeared into the maze.

'Right,' Tyrone was thinking to himself. 'It's simply a matter of keeping on this path and always taking the turning that leads inwards.' Within five minutes, he found himself at his third dead end, thoroughly disorientated and unable to decide which direction he was facing. He stuffed his handkerchief into the hedge, and tried to retrace his steps. Every avenue looked identical. He plunged on, selecting a turning which seemed unfamiliar, but after rounding a couple of corners found himself once more confronted by his handkerchief. There was no one in sight. He decided to cheat and climb the hedge to have a look over. This proved almost impossible as there were no firm footholds, only a line of vertical iron railings embedded in the thin, prickly branches. He thrust one leg deep into the foliage, which scratched at him like tiny fingernails, and then tried to do the same with his right arm. He managed to get both feet off the ground before losing his balance and toppling backwards on to the path, his right leg still entangled in the branches, the ankle twisted painfully. He tried to withdraw it, winced and gave up. He lay back, his free leg propped vertically against the hedge, hands behind his head, gazing at the sun through half-closed eyes. It was completely quiet. Then he noticed the symphony of birdsong, which seemed to have come from nowhere, gradually detach itself from the silence and fill the air. Somewhere in the distance two dogs were barking at each other. A soft breeze was lifting his hair and gently stroking his face. He shut his eyes, enjoying the luxurious warmth, revelling in the absurdity of his position. Slowly he became aware of footsteps. 'Charlotte has come to find me,' he thought, gently disengaging his foot from its leafy snare. There were several small cuts around the ankle which was already beginning to swell. The footsteps grew louder, and a small girl, no more than three, came tripping towards him, her blonde bunches bouncing as she walked.

"Ding dong, ding dong," she said, standing in front of him with her feet apart and her stomach sticking out. She was holding a white knitted duck with a yellow felt beak.

"Hello," said Tyrone affably. "Are you lost too?" He licked his handkerchief, and dabbed up a round bead of blood like a ladybird from his shin. The little girl squatted down on her haunches and watched, fascinated.

"Poor leg," she finally said, patting Tyrone's knee sympathetically, and then skipped off again, half-singing, half-chattering to herself.

"We'd better find your mummy," he called out, hobbling after her. "Wait for me," as her little yellow dress disappeared around the next corner. He limped faster, following the sound of tuneless gibberish as it drifted back to him. Occasionally he caught sight of a flash of yellow. A few minutes later he bumped into Charlotte, who had grown bored of waiting for him and had decided to make her way out. She was carrying the struggling child in her arms.

"Where have you been?" she demanded, handing over the writhing infant, who was reaching out eagerly to Tyrone. "I've been in there ages."

"Lost. How did you get to the middle so quickly?" The little girl nestled against his shoulder contentedly.

"Keeping to the left-hand hedge. You just follow it all the way round."

"How did you know that?"

"I read it somewhere. Of course, once you know the secret, mazes are no fun any more. It's the challenge of getting lost and stumbling around that's important."

"Sure," said Tyrone, flexing his foot.

"Obviously not in your case — I nipped past you at one

point, and saw you trying to climb the hedge. What have you done to your foot anyway?" She noticed that he was walking with some difficulty.

"I left it behind in the branches while the rest of me fell out. It's sprained, I think."

"Serves you right for cheating," said Charlotte, but she knelt down and placed a cool hand on the swelling.

They stood back to make way for a skinny young couple who were draped around each other, and seemed to Charlotte to have about eight arms between them.

"And who are you?" she crowed unconvincingly to the child, who turned away silent and unimpressed. "Where's Mummy?" she tried again. The girl ignored her and began humming, twisting one of her silky bunches round a fat finger.

"Not very talkative, is she?" said Charlotte, irritated that her discomposure with children was transparent even to a three-year-old.

"No," said Tyrone, as the uncooperative child untangled her finger from her hair and poked it into his ear, "I think she's more of a physical communicator."

"Hey!" One of the polybrachial lovers came towards them holding the knitted duck. "Your daughder's drarped this," she said in an American accent. Charlotte and Tyrone looked at one another apologetically and laughed.

Outside the maze, a young woman was crouching over a buggy containing a smooth round baby, tickling its feet with a blade of grass and responding rapturously to its delighted gurgles.

"Isoochycoochyicklefeetiesticklyye-e-e-es," she cooed as the tiny blue and white crocheted bundle waved its legs ecstatically. Catching sight of her daughter cradled in Tyrone's arms, she left the buggy and hurried over.

"There you are," she said, fondly scooping her up and kissing her shining hair. "Thank you." She addressed this to Tyrone and Charlotte, who smiled back fascinated as the child immediately burst into a stream of nonsensical chatter, which the mother answered in the same vein. As the trio

67

moved off, mother and daughter could be heard singing a soft wordless melody, swinging their clasped hands, while cries of pleasure rose like bubbles from the buggy.

Charlotte and Tyrone made their way to the Park, Tyrone still limping, and flopped down in a pool of shade beside the Long Water.

"Isn't this just . . ." Charlotte waved her hand expressively in the direction of the palace.

"Mmmm."

"Days like this are so—"

She was interrupted by a loud shriek as Tyrone tried to whistle through a blade of grass. A sparrow was warbling in the branches above them.

"O for a draught of vintage," said Tyrone. "What did you do with the beer?"

"Left it behind. Did you know that Patrick is thinking of going teetotal?"

"It wouldn't surprise me in the least. It's ever since he met that druid bloke. Eating vegetable juice and raw garlic and grated turnip. Probably poison himself."

"Greg believes that there's nothing that isn't edible provided you slice it thinly enough."

Tyrone spat out some strands of grass. "I think I'd find that Brotherhood mumbo-jumbo pretty hard to swallow, however thinly it was sliced."

"It won't last," Charlotte reassured him. "You know Patrick's craze mentality. One week it's Green politics that will save the world, and the next it's Esperanto. He's always on the lookout for a new cause." She was distracted by the sight of Tyrone's ankle, which was purple and puffy. "You're not going to be able to drive with that foot," she observed.

"Yes I will. I just need to practise walking on it," and he staggered to his feet and headed unsteadily off towards the ornamental gardens. After a couple of tentative circuits of the fountain, he returned to find Charlotte curled up in the grass, fast asleep, her cheek resting on her hand, a serene smile on her face. Tyrone sat down nearby, watching her.

'So pure a thing, so free from mortal taint,' he thought,

touched, as if her going to sleep was somehow a gesture of trust. At the same time he felt jealous.

He tried to remember the last time he had slept like that, safely, peacefully, untroubled by tormented dreams.

The dying fire outside was throwing strange patterns on to the walls of the tent, which was rippling and straining in the wind. Sean crawled through the flap and zipped it closed behind him.

"It's blowing a gale out there. I wouldn't be surprised if we lose the fly sheet."

Tyrone was already in his sleeping bag, lying on his back, reading by the light of a torch. Sean was hunched up, trying to pull on a pair of tracksuit pants.

"Ow," said Tyrone as Sean lost his balance and kicked him in the ribs.

"Shhh." Sean raised his hand. Faintly, over the roar of the wind came the plaintive cry of an owl. "Probably caught a mouse."

"Well, it'll have to defrost it if it's been out in this weather," replied Tyrone, pulling his scarf up around his ears. He was wearing gloves and an extra jumper over normal clothes. Sean was putting on a second pair of socks.

"Do you think we'll make this climb tomorrow?" he panted, struggling into his sleeping bag.

"I don't know." Tyrone switched off the torch. "That wind might be a problem." The fire had gone out, leaving them in pitch darkness. He could hear Sean breathing, but could not actually see him, although they were only inches apart. The wind was shrieking in the trees, beating the tiny tent mercilessly. The ground was as cold and rigid as marble, penetrating groundsheet, fabric and flesh indiscriminately, chilling him to the bone. He tried to wriggle his toes, but without actually touching them couldn't tell whether they were moving.

"Are you awake?" hissed Sean, very close.

"Yes, and I'm bloody freezing."

"So am I. Why don't we both get in one sleeping bag and use the other as a blanket?"

Tyrone fumbled along the side of the tent for the torch and pointed it at Sean, casting a shadow like a reclining giant against the canvas. Sean climbed in beside him, dragging his own sleeping bag across the top of them. It was a tight squeeze. Tyrone could feel Sean's knees against the back of his legs, and an elbow digging into his back, as he tried to work out what to do with his arms. Finally Sean stopped fidgeting.

"Are you comfortable?" Tyrone croaked, hardly daring to acknowledge this new-found intimacy.

"No," came a blast of hot breath on the back of his neck.

'I'll never get off to sleep like this,' Tyrone thought. It only seemed like moments later that he awoke to find the morning sun filling the tent with a luminous orange glow. Sean was still asleep, breathing lightly, clinging on to him like a koala bear. Tyrone lay very still so as not to disturb him, enjoying the warmth and security, as well as a liberating feeling of transgression. The wind had died down during the night and it promised to be a glorious day.

Charlotte opened her eyes. Tyrone was looking through her rather than at her. She sat up and he seemed to start, as if he had forgotten she was there.

"How long have I been asleep?" she asked, pulling her skirt down over her knees, and brushing strands of grass out of her hair.

"An hour or so." Tyrone glanced at his watch.

"Have you just been sitting there?" Charlotte tried and failed to sound casual. Privately, the idea of Tyrone watching her sleep made her feel uncomfortable.

He read her mind. "No, fair Madeline, I haven't been leering at you." He warmed to the subject. "I was going to test the plausibility of that bit from 'The Eve of St Agnes', and lay out a Bacchanalian orgy of lukewarm beer and curling chicken sandwiches, but then I remembered we'd left them

70

in the car." He pulled her to her feet. "Time to go home."

She looked dubiously at his ankle, but said nothing as he walked with obvious discomfort back to the car.

It was already quite dark as they approached Oxford. Tyrone had driven quite slowly on a circuitous back route, trying to avoid any sudden manoeuvres. The road was almost deserted — Charlotte could just see the red lights of the car in front disappearing around a bend, and the line of cats' eyes snaking away into the distance.

"It's been a wonderful day," she was saying, gazing out of the window at the moon. Only the thinnest sliver of rind was showing. Suddenly something dashed out of the hedge into the road. Tyrone saw a pair of terrified yellow eyes in the glare of the headlamps before he slammed his foot down. A searing pain tore up his leg, and he momentarily blacked out. There was a yelp as the car struck the creature, knocking it into the middle of the road. Charlotte had covered her eyes. Tyrone leapt out of the car in horror, his ankle nearly giving way under him. A black labrador puppy lay motionless across the cat's eyes. Charlotte tried to pick it up. It was heavy and limp, its paws flopping over her arms. There was a dark sticky gash above one eye. It had no collar or name tag. Tyrone was squatting in the road with his head in his hands.

"It was an accident," he kept repeating.

"What are we going to do?" Charlotte called from the grass verge where she gently deposited the dog. Tyrone got back in the car, his face grey and trembling. "We can't just dump it here without telling anyone."

"It's dead, for God's sake," he said wildly. "Whatever we do won't make any difference."

"Not to the dog. But to the owner . . ." she protested quietly, sitting back in the car.

"How are we going to find them? There aren't any houses for miles around." He gestured towards the open fields. "It was an accident," he said again, in a broken voice.

"Yes, I know." Charlotte was tearful now. "I know accidents can't be helped. But it's how you behave afterwards that counts."

Tyrone was ashen, his mouth fixed in a tight line. "There's a car coming," he said as a beam of light swept into view behind them. Wincing, he pressed his bad foot down on the accelerator and drove on into the blackness.

Back at College, Charlotte found a letter from her mother. In it was the news she had been dreading.

> Dear Charlie,
> I hope you are looking after yourself, and not working too hard. We will love you whatever you get. I'm afraid I have some bad news. Uncle John died last night, at about 3 a.m. We've all been expecting it but even so it was a shock. At least he is no longer in agony. Your father is going to the funeral on Saturday. I'm not going. We can't afford two train fares to Aberystwyth, and the car is not reliable enough for long journeys any more. Well, I'm sorry not to have any good news. We miss you.
>
> > Lots of love,
> > Mum and Dad

10

PATRICK and Greg were sitting in Boris's garden drinking mint tea and playing a game of Go, when Alison arrived. They were balancing on rickety cane chairs with a dusty wrought-iron table between them, and gazing intently at the board. The warmth of the breeze and the feel of the smooth polished counters had relaxed Patrick into a somnambulistic torpor. Every so often an insect would drop out of the vine which clambered along the trellis above their heads, and land on the board. Greg would remove it carefully and place it on a leaf, or blow it gently away, before resuming the game. Ilsa was baking a banana loaf in the kitchen, and the hot sweet smell came drifting out into the garden.

Patrick had reached an impasse. Wherever he placed his black counter, Greg's white ones would still be able to surround him. Greg tipped the teapot upside down and emptied the soggy leaves on to the lawn. Picking a fresh sprig of mint from a terracotta urn beside the French doors, he took the teapot back to the kitchen to be refilled. Patrick could hear the slap of his sandals against the path. They had not spoken a word for over half an hour — there had been a tacit agreement that the game would proceed in silence.

'Greg has obviously been concentrating harder than I have,' Patrick thought. He found himself easily distracted. A robin bounced towards him and stopped a few feet away, an enquiring look in his bright black eyes. He could hear the faint clack of Boris's typewriter. Greg returned with the tea and two slices of Ilsa's loaf, warm and steaming on the earthenware plate. Today every sound, every texture seemed to have been designed purely to contribute to Patrick's feeling of exquisite well-being, from the cool weight of the counters to the soft singing coming from the kitchen.

'If only every day could be like this,' he thought. He knew that tomorrow he would have to return to his books and the relentless drill of reading, theorising, illustrating and re-writing that his doctorate had become.

Not necessarily, Greg's tranquil expression seemed to say. There is another way.

Patrick placed his crucial disc casually on the board. Greg retaliated instantly, enclosing a little cluster of black counters and impounding them. He smiled apologetically. The singing stopped and was replaced by an exchange of female voices. Ilsa showed Alison through the French windows, brushing cobwebs off the door frame with her apron as she passed.

"Hello," said Alison cheerfully, her voice breaking the men's silence. Greg stood up to offer her a chair. She was holding a plastic bag full of old clothes. "I thought I might find you here," she went on, sitting on Greg's empty seat while he squatted on the doorstep. "I'm collecting clothes for Archie. I've already got Tyrone's old grey coat and those awful baggy violet trousers he used to wear. I've taken one of Oliver's cardigans too. He doesn't know yet. I was wondering if Boris might have anything to spare."

"Ilsa will love you," Patrick said. "She's always trying to get rid of his worn-out stuff, but as soon as she threatens to throw something out he suddenly manifests this senti-mental attachment to it."

A moment later Ilsa reappeared, carrying an armful of miscellaneous garments which she dumped in the middle of the floor. Boris had obviously heard her rummaging around upstairs, as he had emerged from the Time Room and was hovering anxiously around the bundle of cast-offs.

"There are these tatty corduroys you never wear." Ilsa addressed him, holding up a pair of sagging, fawn trousers, slightly worn around the seat. She folded them up and handed them to Alison.

"But I use those for . . . for decorating," Boris protested, retrieving them. "I can't do without those."

"You never do any decorating," Ilsa corrected him, "and if you did you would never do anything as sensible as change your clothes first." But he clung persistently to the trousers.

"Now this jacket can definitely go." She brushed the dust off a battered leather flying-jacket with a thick, sheepskin lining. "It's that awful stiff thing which stands in the corner by itself," she explained to Boris, who seized it, outraged.

"This is a part of my history," he wailed, stroking the woolly lining fondly as if it were a pet. "It's nearly fifty years old."

Alison was embarrassed at the disturbance she was causing. Patrick and Greg had abandoned their game and were watching the proceedings through the open doors.

"What's this? What's this?" Boris was saying with an air of panic, as Ilsa produced a chunky fairisle pullover. He groped at it frantically. "But you knitted me this, Ilsa. I can't part with this. I remember you winding the skeins around my hands. It took you all winter to make."

"Yes, and it was summer by the time I'd finished it so you only wore it twice. You said it made your neck itch. Well, you certainly won't need these again," she said decisively, displaying an ancient pair of solid black walking boots. "We're far too old and lazy to go hiking now."

"Oh, I remember these," her husband cried delightedly, feeling their weight and sturdiness. "Craftsmanship," he said, fondling them. "Not like this modern rubbish."

Ilsa raised her eyes ceilingwards and winked at Alison. "Alison must think you very mean, dear, refusing to part with anything for poor Mr Harris."

Boris looked downcast for a moment, then brightened.

"Here you are," he said, struggling out of his new sports jacket and sleeveless pullover. "He can have these. I don't need them. I'd much rather keep these old things instead," he mumbled from within the jumper. "When you are blind

75

new clothes are nothing but a burden," as his head emerged, his white hair bristling with static. He fought his way into the flying jacket, slipped the boots on, and threw the corduroys over one arm.

"I won't embarrass the ladies," he said, and clumped stiffly out of the room like an astronaut.

Alison was looking doubtfully at the pile of Boris's discarded clothing.

"I can't take these," and she handed them back to Ilsa. "They're brand new."

"No, do have them. Boris has said so, and you must always take him at his word."

Alison bit her lip and looked at Patrick. "Oh, dear," she said. "I only wanted cast-offs, and I appear to have stripped Boris to his underwear."

"You should be a charity fund raiser. They need ruthless people like you."

"Isn't it strange how everybody hoards cupboards full of clutter which they never use and wouldn't miss, and yet can't be persuaded to part with?" mused Ilsa.

"Everybody except Greg, of course," said Alison, giving him a sly look.

Greg smiled indulgently. "And Mr Harris presumably." He found the comparison of himself with a tramp quite pleasing.

"How is Mr Harris?" Ilsa asked Alison, folding Boris's spurned garments into a neat pile.

"He's coming along fine. He had a good wash the other day, but he still refuses to cut off his beard. I've just left him demolishing Rosie's shed."

"Does she know?" enquired Patrick.

"Oh yes. She wants it out of the way so she can grow vegetables. It was rotten anyway."

She had called round to see Archie that morning, and found him sitting on the shed roof ripping planks out with a claw hammer. He was wearing a clean checked shirt and a pair of paint-splattered jeans which Rosie had found in the attic. He waved at Alison as she approached. Apart from his hair and beard, which were still matted and bushy, he looked

76

positively respectable, like a slightly hairy husband doing the weekend gardening chores.

It was the first time she had seen him since Rosie had smuggled him into her squash club and forced him to take a shower.

"Hello, Pygmalion," Rosie greeted her, emerging from the shed, carrying a pile of mildewed wooden seed trays. "Isn't he good?" she gestured towards the silent figure above them. "Do you know he's worked out this fraudulent method of claiming housing rebate, without me getting penalised for tax."

The arrangement seemed to be working. Rosie did not make any money out of Archie, but he helped out with odd jobs and kept the garden tidy. He had been a carpenter at some stage during his career, and had already mended her dividing fence and wooden picnic table.

"At least having a man around the place might deter aggressive husbands from harassing you. That must be a comfort," Alison had said without thinking.

Rosie looked at her in amazement. "Alison, some of the women here have been victims of male violence since they were kids. One can hardly reassure them that things are going to be okay now because we've got 'a man around the place'. As it happens," she went on, seeing Alison's face fall, "I find him a very soothing lodger. He doesn't interfere with my life, he never contradicts me and he does all my nasty chores without complaint or payment. In fact, he is probably most men's idea of the perfect wife." She gave a screech. "Oh Rose, thou art sick."

Archie was lowering himself through the bared ribs of the roof into the main body of the shed. There was already a large pile of splintered planks on the grass beside them.

"Shall I carry on?" he asked in his soft, slightly rasping voice, wiping the film of sweat off his face with a grubby handkerchief.

"No, have a rest." Rosie slapped him heartily on the shoulder. "I'll get you a drink. Orange all right?"

He nodded. He had not had so much as a sniff of alcohol for the last fortnight.

"How are you?" Alison bit back the impulse to say "we", and knelt down on the grass next to him. She found herself constantly having to guard against treating him like an imbecile. He was so apologetic, so vacant, so devoid of any personal pride, that she frequently noticed a simpering tone creeping into her voice when she spoke to him. She would catch herself using the sort of clichés normally reserved for the old, the young and the sick. 'Imagine he is your father,' she told herself. That did not help either, as she had no experience in that sphere, her own father having gone absent without leave before she was born.

"You look a lot better."

"Bit down," he replied, avoiding her eye, tearing the petals off a daisy.

"Why?" Alison asked in dismay. "Everything is going to be fine now."

"Oh . . ." he shrugged. "Bit down, that's all."

"But I've got some good news for you." She tried to sound enthusiastic, but could tell she was coming across as bumptious and patronising. "There was a card in the newsagent's window this morning, asking about a gardener for two afternoons a week. You could do that."

It was the sort of job that Alison would never have dreamed of doing herself, yet for some reason she assumed it would give him a surge of self-esteem.

He forced a smile and looked up at her earnest face. "You're a nice young lady but you're wasting your time worrying about me," and he struggled to his feet and resumed his demolition work.

Alison decided to call the number on the newsagent's card anyway, and persuade whoever answered to take Archie on for a trial period. He would be hopeless on the phone, giving up at the first hint of resistance. Then she would call on Tyrone, Patrick and Boris to collect some men's clothing. 'Finally,' she told herself, 'perhaps I will get some work done.' Recently she had taken to getting up in the middle of the night and sneaking into the spare room to snatch a few extra hours' revision. It was a good system, as she was always restless and wakeful in the early hours, worrying about the impending exams or peering beyond into the dense fog which seemed to obscure her view of the future.

Now here she was at Boris's and another working day was slipping away. She stood up to leave, picking up her bulging carrier bag. Ilsa put a hand on her arm as if to detain her.

"It is so good to have everyone here," she smiled shyly at the three young people. "Perhaps, Boris, we could persuade them to stay to dinner." Boris had returned, still wearing his boots and flying jacket.

"Of course you must all stay," he said as though the alternative was inadmissible. "There is no pleasure in the world like sharing a meal with friends."

Patrick accepted with alacrity, Greg with his usual composure. Alison felt torn. She desperately wanted to stay. Boris and Ilsa's house felt like a haven of comfort and sanity compared to ... she could not complete the comparison, she hardly dared think what she meant. Oliver would not understand her desire to stay anywhere without him. She had promised to be back by six. She had even defrosted a whole chicken. Besides, she had used the urgency of work as an excuse to avoid so many of his recreational suggestions that she felt this one lapse from her study programme would invalidate all future demands for privacy.

Patrick and Greg had resumed their game of Go. Patrick was losing, and Greg was staring at him with his enigmatic, penetrating eyes. Alison felt a pang of exclusion which strengthened her determination to stay.

"Can I use the phone?" she called out.

"Of course," replied Boris and Ilsa in unison.

She decided to call Oliver and tell him that she would be working late in the library. A plausible lie was nothing but an economical short-cut, far simpler than justifying her right to a little independence. 'Besides,' she told herself, 'I am entitled to lie to Oliver, because he would react so unreasonably if I told him the truth.' She felt his irrational possessiveness not only excused her deceit, it actually decreed it. She was glad Charlotte was not there to witness such blatant casuistry. Charlotte always laughed at the way Alison never confronted an issue directly, but sidled up to it from an oblique angle. It was almost as if Alison would sooner put herself in the wrong than be forced to crush Oliver in an argument. There would be something so despicable about him blustering ahead with a palpably unsound argument. She preferred to compromise her own integrity rather than witness such an ugly sight.

"Hello," an apologetic tone already creeping into her voice.

"Hello," came the cautious reply. "Is that you?"

She was glad she had caught him mid-tutorial. The conversation would have to be brief.

"Oliver, I'm just ringing to say that I won't be back for dinner tonight."

"Oh," came the crestfallen reply. "I was going to make us a trifle. I've bought all the bits to go on it."

Alison could imagine his tutee looking at him in astonishment and almost laughed. She lowered her voice, hoping that the rest of the household were out of earshot.

"The thing is, I've got hold of this really useful library book, but it is on someone else's reserve list, so I'll have to read it tonight. I'll grab something to eat and be back after ten." The lies slipped smoothly out. It worried her how easy it was to come up with such deliberate untruths, how readily she almost began believing them herself.

"You poor thing — you're working too hard. You should give yourself an evening off, go out with some friends." Concern made him lower his guard for an instant, before he remembered he was not alone. He cleared his throat hastily. "Well, I'm busy now. Thank you for ringing. Goodbye," and he hung up.

Alison felt cheated. 'Typical,' she thought. 'Trust him to be magnanimous. Now I feel terrible.'

The game of Go was still in progress. Greg, confident of victory, had relaxed his concentration, allowing Patrick to make a comeback. Gradually Patrick began to amass a pile of white counters. At last he felt he was getting to grips with strategy. Alison stood behind him, looking over his shoulder. It did not take her long to work out the rules, but it was not exactly, she decided, a game for spectators.

Ilsa came out and spread a red tartan rug on the lawn. Alison stretched out on it, watching Ilsa lead Boris around the garden to smell the flowers. A lilac bush, suffocated with heavy blooms like bunches of silvery grapes, was leaning against the creaking fence. Boris thrust his face amongst the flowers and breathed rapturously.

The game was over and the counters returned to their box. Stalemate had finally been declared: with each turn, Greg and Patrick had become increasingly ponderous and analytical, and the game threatened to go on all evening. Patrick joined Alison on the rug, looking forward to a whole evening of her company. She was absent-mindedly fingering a daisy.

"He loves me," she said.

"Who does?" said Patrick.

"The chief examiner, hopefully. He loves me not," as another petal floated to the ground.

Greg had wandered down to the herb garden and was filling his pockets with sprigs of thyme and sage.

"Would you like me to put some cuttings in water for you?" Ilsa asked.

"No, no. We have some bushes back in our own garden, thank you. I just like to smell them. Sometimes when I have a headache or feel tired, I tie a bunch of fresh lavender or thyme around my neck and breathe in the scent. It never fails."

"It feels unusually warm," Boris interrupted. He was still wearing the fairisle jersey and worn corduroys. "Is this attributable to the heat of the sun or the inappropriateness of my costume?" he asked the company in general.

"Both, I think," said Greg, squinting upwards.

"Perhaps we could eat outside?" Ilsa had picked a few bunches of lilac blossom and went indoors to find a vase. She reappeared a moment later carrying a porcelain chamberpot filled with water, in which she arranged the blooms. She examined the brick barbecue on the patio, removing the blackened aluminium foil and tipping the ashes over the flowerbed. "We can cook the casserole over this," she said to Alison and Patrick. "So much nicer than being cooped up indoors."

"Can I cut anything up for you?" Patrick stood up and followed her into the kitchen. Greg took his place on the rug beside Alison, sitting cross-legged with closed eyes, as if meditating. A wavering duet of 'True Love' drifted towards them through the window. Alison cleared her throat. Greg, aware that this was a prelude to conversation, looked up and raised his eyebrows at her.

"Is this one of your days off?" She could not think of an alternative opener, but wanted him to talk, to reveal what, if anything, lay beneath his chilly exterior. She found the idea of his celibacy a little threatening, as if it represented a personal rebuff. She remembered Brother Damian, the young priest who had taught Religious Studies at her private girls' school. Her fifth form confederates had interpreted his unassailable chastity as a deliberate affront to their charms and had waged a ruthless campaign of flirtation and innu-endo. His frosty indifference was encountered at first with incredulity, finally forcing them to conclude that the male libido was not as volatile as literature had seemed to imply.

Although she had been deflated at the time, seven years on Alison supposed that she ought to be grateful. Brother Damian had after all been an unprompted champion of the principle that accountability for the male sexual urge lay with men rather than women.

"I don't have days on and off as such," Greg was explaining patiently. "That leads to precisely the sort of self-division that the Brotherhood denounces. I pity people who go off at nine every morning and work until five at something which bears no relation to the way they live the rest of their lives."

"For you and I have a guardian angel . . ." crooned Patrick and Ilsa in the background.

Greg pressed on, undeterred. "Think of the guy whose job

82

it is to put those little plastic motorbikes into Christmas crackers. How does he cope? By splitting himself in half, sending an automaton into work five days a week, and saving the real person for weekends."

Alison nodded. It was impossible to make light conversation with Greg. He was so remote, so humourless. 'He makes all these claims for humility, but he never wastes an opportunity to preach the superiority of his own lifestyle,' she thought.

"I prefer to see my life as a continuum," he was warming to his subject now.

"But you must have to do boring jobs occasionally," she said.

"I don't regard them as boring. All my duties are necessary and self-imposed, and I enjoy them as much as any other activity, so a day off has no real meaning."

"What do you mean, 'you enjoy them all equally'?" Alison asked suspiciously. "Don't you prefer reading a good book or talking with friends to . . ." she wrinkled her brow, trying to think of the most dismal of domestic duties, ". . . washing up, or emptying the dustbin?" She was sure she had him trapped there.

"No, I don't. A chore only becomes a chore because of the attitude of the person doing it. If you consider washing dishes as a boring, time-consuming task which only delays you from doing something more exciting, then naturally it is going to be a negative experience. But if you think of its purpose, and its merits, and the consequences of not doing it, then it becomes a positive pleasure." He did not bat an eyelid as he said this.

"I don't believe it," laughed Alison.

"Think how depressing it would be to eat off plates all streaked and spattered with food, and how good it feels to see them clean and shining. It's so satisfying watching all the grease and muck being washed away down the plug-hole. In fact, now I come to think of it, it is probably even better than reading a book or talking to friends, because as well as its aesthetic advantages, you always end up with a finished product." He gave her the benefit of an ironic smile.

"I thought for a moment you were serious," she exclaimed, throwing a handful of grass at him. He brushed it away calmly.

"I am."

"You can't be," she protested. "I know I'm not Dorothy Parker, but it does come as a blow to my ego to think that you would rather wash a bowl of greasy plates than have a chat with me."

"There you are then," he said with quiet triumph. "It's your ego which is the problem. Anyway I didn't say I would prefer washing up. I merely said it was probably better."

Patrick and Ilsa had brought a heavy wooden board and a couple of sharp knives out on to the terrace, and were sitting at the table chopping vegetables from a wicker basket between them.

Alison would not give up. "Patrick. As a pastime, do you prefer talking to me or dicing vegetables?" She looked at him across the rockery.

He put his head on one side. "Depends what you were talking about." Greg let out an uncharacteristic laugh. "If it was the double helix, or the rise of the yen, I might stick with this onion." Pulling a face at him she turned back to Greg.

"But you must have some hierarchy of enjoyment. Everyone does. It's the only thing which drives us all on, isn't it, the pursuit of pleasure?"

"What's the pecking order in your aristocracy of the senses then?" He was lying flat on his back with his hands behind his head. The light was reflecting off his glasses, turning them into dazzling white moons.

This was tricky. "Reading a good book, having a meal with friends, travelling, shopping . . . somewhere near the bottom would be going to the dentist and eating oysters."

"What?" The brilliant discs flashed at her. "You prefer a good book to a good life, and you think I'm strange."

"I didn't mean that exactly." She covered her face with her hands. "I'm still sure I'm right, though."

"There is no right or wrong in this argument, is there?" interrupted Patrick.

"Yes, there is," she insisted. "It's not just that I don't believe that you can enjoy all experiences equally, it's more that I don't believe Greg believes it."

He shrugged his shoulders.

"For instance, if you don't admit any preferences, how did you come to the decision to stay for a meal here rather than go home? Surely that involved a value judgement."

Greg refused to get irritated by her persistent scepticism, which riled her even more.

"What are you trying to do, Alison?" he said with a charming look of resignation. "Do you want me to crumble and admit that I'm wrong? You aren't interested in pursuing the truth. You just want to win."

She blushed for a moment, as if she was being rebuked by a teacher. He was right. She had wanted to batter him with questions until he surrendered, to feel that moment of triumph. It was barbaric. With a heroic effort, she said, "Of course you're right, Greg. If you say all pleasures are equal to you, then they are and that's that. Anyway, it's none of my bloody business." The strain of such a display of self-abnegation almost choked her.

Greg was spared having to reply to this little speech, as Patrick's injudicious use of methylated spirit on the barbecue caused an unexpected diversion.

Patrick gave a yell as the coals exploded into flame, and leapt backwards clutching his eyebrows. Greg was at his side in an instant, before Alison had even stood up. He seemed to have flown through the air, his skirt gliding across the grass without making contact with the ground. He was pulling Patrick's hand down from his eyes, saying "Let me see. Let me see." Ilsa came running out with a flannel, which Patrick groped for without looking up and applied to his face. He was shaking. The others glanced at each other nervously. Boris appeared at the French windows, a look of concern on his face. Patrick was making a strange gurgling noise, which gave way as he removed the flannel from his streaked, sooty face to maniacal laughter, and continued until everyone including the baffled Boris had joined in.

"Oh . . . oh . . ." Alison wiped her eyes.

Greg had thrown his head back and his clear laugh rang out like a bell.

"You silly fool." Ilsa was leaning on Patrick for support, pressing her stomach to relieve a stitch. Patrick was still bent double and gasping. "You had us all worried. We thought you had been blinded." Patrick felt his eyebrows cautiously. A few singed hairs crumbled away as he brushed them, leaving them looking sparse and patchy like a mangy fox fur. This set everyone off again.

By the time Patrick had washed his face and trimmed the frizzled ends of his hair into something approaching a fringe, an air of calm had descended on the party. Ilsa had thrown a stiff white cloth over the wrought-iron table, and set the chamberpot in the centre. The flames had died back and the coals were beginning to glow orange. Ilsa heaved the cast iron casserole of vegetables on to the barbecue and gave them a stir with a long wooden spoon. It was stained and yellow with saffron, and had a scorch mark across the handle where it had been left lying against the side of a hot pan. Within seconds the onions had started to hiss.

It was still daylight, but Ilsa lit a couple of white candles and melted them into their brass holders, dripping blobs of wax like thick tears on to the concrete of the terrace. Greg and Patrick brought out extra chairs, and Alison laid the table, pulling faces at herself in the spoons. Ilsa was presiding over the pot, adding chopped parsley and coriander and grinding pepper from a heavy marble mill. Greg sat down at the table and began pounding garlic cloves with a pestle and mortar. The wood was smooth and polished and made a pleasing 'clock clock' sound as he worked. Boris brought out a bottle of the neighbours' home-made strawberry wine, and poured four glasses without spilling a drop. He fetched Greg a glass of water with wedges of orange and lemon floating in it. They were all sitting around the table by now, except Ilsa who was still maintaining a vigil over the pot.

A sweet, earthy smell of garlic and simmering vegetables was fanned gently across the table by the breeze.

Alison sipped the wine. It was surprisingly dry, not the unpalatable syrup she had been expecting, and it tasted distinctly of strawberries. She took a gulp and immediately felt loose and light-headed. It occurred to her that she had not eaten since breakfast, and she pushed her glass away hastily, only to find it being refilled by Patrick.

When the casserole had been bubbling vigorously for some time, Ilsa took it off the coals and rested it on a basket-weave mat in the middle of the table. Then she went back to the kitchen and returned carrying a freshly baked loaf in a tin. She tipped it out on to a plate with a thud. The crust was dark brown and studded with seeds. Greg shut his eyes for a few seconds as if in prayer, while Boris gingerly broke the loaf into five, wincing as the steam burnt his fingers. They all helped themselves to bowls of the stew which they ate with spoons, Boris tearing his bread into chunks and drowning them in the juice. Alison devoured her bread with indecent speed, hoping to blot up the wine. No one spoke, as if there was a sanctity about the meal which had to be preserved. The only sounds were the slop of the bread in the stew and the scrape of spoon against earthenware. The sun was nearly set, streaking the sky with violet. Ilsa's soft oval face glowed gold in the candlelight, which sent flickering yellow lights over the table, across Greg's sharp cheekbones and into the shimmering blackness of Alison's eyes.

Patrick felt as though he had stumbled unawares into a Rembrandt and was surrounded by silent, fleshy shapes, their faces brilliantly illuminated but everything dark and shadowy beyond. Or perhaps, he thought, he had died and been transported to some other world, where the demands of French puppet theatre had no meaning, and where there was an unconditional supply of food for body and soul.

Ilsa wiped her mouth with a napkin and smoothed the loose strands of hair back into her bun before scraping her chair backwards and standing up. Everyone remained transfixed in the candlelight. The breeze had died down and there was not a noise or a movement anywhere. Alison found she was holding her breath. No one wanted to be the first to ripple the smooth dark pool of silence, so they merely sat, mesmerised, until Ilsa returned with a bottle of Calvados and four small glasses, which she handed to Alison.

"Can I tempt anyone?" Alison whispered, holding it up. The liquid looked richly yellow, and smelled old and musty. The label was striped with sticky drips to which generations of dust and fluff had clung.

Only Greg abstained. Patrick took a sniff of the liqueur and the sharp fumes burnt the inside of his nostrils. Alison was feeling pleasantly drunk. Boris swallowed his in one draught, then excused himself and disappeared through the French windows.

'How strange', thought Patrick, 'that a blind man should feel so at home with silence.' A moment later the smooth creamy notes of the clarinet came spilling out on to the terrace. It was 'Patrick's Song'.

It had been indescribably beautiful on the piano, but the haunting voice of the clarinet gave it a new quality of ghostliness. Patrick felt as if it was a secret communication from Boris to him — a gesture of solidarity winging its way invisibly across the stillness; a requiem for a perfect day. He allowed himself a private, privileged smile.

"What a lovely tune," Alison burst out, drink making her unusually voluble.

'Was that it?' Patrick wondered. 'Was that all that could be sincerely said, without the words taking over and falsifying everything.' He supposed so. He stood up as Boris returned. "I must be going soon. Thank you for the meal. Perhaps I could stay and wash up?" He began to gather the bowls into an unsteady pile. Greg stopped him.

"Let me do it." He smiled generously in Alison's direction, before looking back into Patrick's eyes. "I assure you it would be a pleasure."

It was way past eleven by the time Alison reached Salisbury Street. 'How am I going to explain this?' she asked herself hysterically. The library closed at ten. The bedroom light was still on. As she pushed the side gate open a cat leapt off the fence into her path, making her drop the bicycle with a clatter. Swearing under her breath, she locked the bicycle in the shed and then stood on the doorstep fumbling for the key in the dark, getting colder and more irritated by the second. It had slipped right to the bottom of the bag of clothes; she could feel it through the taut plastic. In a chattering frenzy she finally tipped out the contents on to the step, retrieved the key and kicked the pile through the open door into the kitchen. By this time, several pretexts for her late homecoming had occurred to her. She remembered the first rule of deceit. Never make more than one excuse. 'I met Charlotte in the library at ten, and went back to her room for a quick glass of Calvados.' That would also explain her state of semi-intoxication, and the reek of apples on her breath.

She clicked the light on. On the kitchen table, wrapped in transparent film, was the roast chicken she had defrosted. It had one leg and a small sliver of breast missing. He had even stuffed it. The thought of Oliver cooking a whole chicken to eat by himself, in that huge empty house, struck Alison as the epitome of loneliness and desolation. A lump came to her throat. He had saved her the breast too. He always gave her the best bits — the burnt top layer of beef, the pork crackling. She opened the fridge. Inside was the other half of the trifle he had mentioned making, sherry and fruit juice leaking out of the sponge, a semi-circle of glacé cherries and a flurry of chopped almonds and angelica embedded in the cream. There was something so touching and pathetic about these remains, these tokens of the reluctant solitary, that it almost choked her. It was as if Oliver could not bear to acknowledge even one evening's isolation but persisted, against all logic, in cooking for two. That was one of the worst things about divorce, he had told her early on in their relationship. Eating alone. He had even confessed to buying a supply of milkshake meal substitutes, so that he could swig one down, standing up in the kitchen.

This bypassed the whole dismal process of sitting down alone at an empty table, listening to the scrape of his own cutlery and the click of his own jaw.

Alison crept up the stairs and into the bedroom, guilt elevating him in her mind from the role of extravagant cook to that of tragic hero. The tragic hero was sitting up in bed, wearing cotton jersey pyjamas and blowing on a glass of hot lemon. This was too much. Tears welled up out of her eyes.

"What's the matter, darling?" He put down his glass and held out his arms. "You're working too hard."

She flopped on to her knees beside him and let him stroke her hair and shoulders, while she sniffled into a tissue, unable to speak.

"I missed you," he said, at which her crying increased. Then reaching past her to the bedside table, he picked up a small navy box and pressed it into her hand. "Alison, let's . . . let's get engaged."

Overwhelmed by a temporary sense of Oliver's vulnerability, and her own unworthiness, she found herself sobbing, "Yes, yes," into the duvet, and clinging even more tightly around his waist as if some jealous hand would otherwise prise them apart.

11

ALISON, predictably, woke up with a headache, a nauseous feeling in her stomach, and an unfocussed sense of anxiety. She propped herself up gently, wincing, and caught sight of the tiny box containing the even tinier diamond ring which Oliver had presented to her after his declaration the night before. It had been far too small. Only a child could have worn it. The source of her discomfort located, she sank back on to the pillows and lay there dry-eyed.

"What have you done?" a small voice in her head kept prodding, and this time it refused to be silenced. "What have you done?"

Charlotte found herself a double seat on the Reading train, and spread out her bag and coat to deter fellow travellers from sitting next to her. She liked going on trains; it was a good place for serious thinking, and it infuriated her that she frequently seemed to act as a magnet for the most intense and persistent conversationalists. She had had conversations about the most bizarre things on trains. Young men and one woman had propositioned her, middle-aged women confided in her about their daughters, daughters about their mothers. She had discussed everything from mastectomy to the greenhouse effect, split ends to socialism. She was also hopeless at assessing potential neighbours. She remembered the poetical-looking youth who had turned out to be an inveterate lecher, and the mousy-looking woman whom she had instantly dismissed as uninteresting but who had kept her entertained for the whole journey with stories of her work as a jazz singer.

Today she wanted to be alone. A large woman opposite was wearing a pink jogging suit, and looked like a human blancmange. She was reading a romantic novel. On the cover was a woman in a plunging period costume of indeterminate century, in the implacable grip of an equally historically-indistinct man. The woman became aware of Charlotte's scrutiny and looked up suspiciously. Charlotte took refuge in *Frankenstein*. Unless you kept a book open, people assumed you were ready for a chat.

She was not going to the funeral itself, but all the same her mother's letter had been a coded summons. Mr Rowley would go on behalf of the family, and Charlotte would remain behind to comfort her mother and be comforted. This was Charlotte's first real encounter with death. Two of her grandparents had died before she was born, and the other two were still robust and healthy. But she had known Uncle John, and his perpetual absence would make a difference. His stern voice, wildly unkempt hair and withering irony had terrified her as a child, but in the last few years she had begun to understand him, to look forward to his visits, and to see him as something more than just the unpredictable dispenser of sweets or sarcasm. She regretted that she had not made an effort to get to know him better, to write or visit more often. She had spent one night crying into her pillow, and had risen the next morning in a mood of etiolated resignation. Accustoming herself to the idea of never seeing him again still left her facing the question of death itself. For someone with little or no religious sense it was a crucial issue. 'Death is the only certainty in life,' she said to herself dramatically, as fields, houses and churches flew past the window, 'therefore ...' She could not work out the second half of the equation. Death is inevitable, therefore life is not worth living? Or was it the other way round — life is worth living because death is inevitable? She remembered lying in bed as a child, looking at the silhouette of the plane tree against the moon and deliberately petrifying herself with thoughts about the appalling finality of death. 'No more Mum, no more Dad, no more Rory, no more holidays, no more netball, no more television, no more anything, ever,' she would silently chant, working herself into a state of wide-eyed terror. Such black nothingness was beyond the powers of the imagination to grasp. It was not like other thoughts, which could be held up, turned over and cut up into manageable chunks. It was vast, dark and empty, and the more one thought about it, the bigger it grew. It could only be described in terms of what it was not, and that was simply not good enough for a hungry mind. The Junior Astronomers' Club had provided her, along with its quarterly newsletter, with the perfect metaphor for death. The Black Hole. An unfathomable unexplorable one-way system, sucking everything inexorably towards its bodiless jaws.

Mr Rowley always said that the great thing about death was that rather than being deprived of the joys of life, one was really only deprived of one's faculty for registering deprivation. An everlasting anaesthetic.

"45, 46, 47 . . . If you have children, you live on through them . . . 48, 49, 50," her mother had said one day, counting stitches. She was not normally given to voicing personal beliefs like that, which was why Charlotte had remembered it. Was that why parents were so reluctant to see their children growing old? she wondered, and why as soon as their adulthood became inevitable, began badgering them to produce grandchildren? It explained too why grandparents were always so shockingly partisan, seeing their descendants as a means of surrogate immortality, a way of keeping one foot in the door from beyond the grave.

A woman was walking unsteadily up the aisle, propelling a toddler towards the toilet. Her husband was following behind her, leading a girl of eight or nine who was wearing a white dress with black cats running around the border.

"How long will we be staying with Nanny?" she was asking, tugging despondently at his sleeve.

"Not long, darling," he replied, ruffling her hair, which she immediately smoothed down again with flat hands. He rummaged in his pocket and brought out a crumpled bag of sweets and popped one in her mouth.

Charlotte, watching all this with interest, suddenly caught the strong, unmistakable smell of cough candy. Cough candy. It was like a scented breeze wafting down the years from her own childhood, sweeping up memories from oblivion and buffeting her with them. Going to visit grandparents; Saturday morning at the sweetshop under the railway bridge; getting up at four in the morning to drive to Devon for the summer holidays, suitcases strapped to the roof-rack, enough food in the picnic basket to furnish a wedding reception. It had seemed like a journey of global proportions, that annual pilgrimage to Ilfracombe, necessitating such an unhallowed hour of departure. And yet one could now do the drive in three hours. Had the country's road systems improved so dramatically in the last twelve years? Charlotte wondered, or had it all been a conspiracy by her parents, this insistence on the gruelling inaccessibility of Devon, to make things more exciting for her and Rory. She had her suspicions. For a split second she recaptured that sense of breathless, childish excitement at setting out on holiday; the clenched fist of happiness in the stomach. Sometimes she felt that adulthood, that much longed-for and envied state, was really an expulsion into a world of comparatively woolly and tranquillised emotions. She thought of recent outings with her parents. "Isn't this fun?" they would repeat. "How exciting." "I *am* enjoying this." But with each assertion of enthusiasm it became more apparent that this was a sadly diluted version of the real exhilaration that as a family they had once felt. Perhaps that was why Christmas was always such a disappointment nowadays. There was an air of simulated jollity about it; the way they all drank excessively, wore stupid hats, pulled crackers and let off little plastic

94

things which went bang and spat coloured paper strands over the turkey. It was as if they were all engaged in a futile tribal ritual to ward off the demons of indifference. What had once been her favourite day now seemed the saddest. It made her want to cry.

The blancmange woman opposite put her book in her handbag and took out a brush matted with dusty hair. She picked off the offending clump, rolled it into a ball, and was about to drop it surreptitiously on to the floor when she caught Charlotte looking at her disapprovingly. Eventually the woman gave up, giving her hair a couple of desultory strokes and then impaling the ball of hair back on the brush. People stood up and retrieved their baggage from the overhead frames. READING READING READING— flashed past in black and white, illegible at first but gradually becoming clearer.

The Rowleys' house was only a fifteen-minute walk from the station, but Charlotte felt lazy and decided to take a taxi. She asked the driver to drop her off at the end of the road so she could approach the house on foot. To her parents, taking taxis fell within the same bracket of financial prodigality as gambling. They belonged to the generation which believed a mortgage to be a millstone around the neck, and who refused to own credit cards on moral grounds. As a concession to thrift Charlotte did not tip the driver. Alison always tipped heavily, everyone from incompetent waiters to disfiguring hairdressers, because, Charlotte suspected, she wanted to be universally liked. Charlotte decided that the gratitude of a balding, tattooed cab-driver was something she could afford to do without, and gave him the exact fare before springing out of the car.

'I must keep calm when they ask me what I intend to do after Finals. I must not, today of all days, get irritable when Mother asks me if I'm eating properly,' she told herself, as she walked down the road. She rehearsed other possible scenarios. 'I must not let them give me any more money. I must not refuse a home-made biscuit. I must not swear.'

Predictably, Mrs Rowley was sweeping the front doorstep as Charlotte approached the house. When one of her offspring was expected, she always stationed herself at some convenient vantage point in the front garden in order to spot them at the earliest opportunity. She did not like to look as if she was watching out for them, so she occupied herself with some unnecessary task, sweeping away non-existent dust or clacking the shears above an already immaculate hedge. Charlotte knew the artifice of this routine, and her mother knew she knew it, but it continued nevertheless.

Mrs Rowley's eyes, small and red from recent crying, brightened as Charlotte gave her a cheerful wave and ran up the path to hug her.

"Hello, darling, lovely to see you," came her mother's muffled voice from the depth of a woolly embrace. "You've lost weight."

Charlotte tried not to rise to this. "I knew you'd say that. Anyway I haven't," and she disengaged herself, and went indoors. She was glad, but not surprised, to see that her mother was not wearing black — but then her side of the family had always known how to do a good funeral. At Mrs Rowley's father's funeral, before Charlotte was born, Aunty Wendy had realised that it would probably be the last time the whole family was together, and had arranged for a photographer to come along.

Inside, the hall looked familiar and welcoming. Its design and ornaments had remained unchanged for the past twenty years. There was a hideous portrait of a robust matron in a grey dress, which was supposed to be a family heirloom and was only kept because it was reputedly worth a bit. Charlotte had shocked her grandparents by once suggesting that they sold it and used the money to buy a decent stair carpet. She still could not comprehend the logic of keeping something grotesque, just because it was valuable, if one had no intention of ever selling it.

There was the old bakelite telephone, a splendid heavy object which, unlike the modern plastic versions, could do real damage if dropped on someone's foot; the red carpet, of course, with its swirling, curling pattern, specially chosen for its ability to disguise stains, footprints and trodden-in food. Beside the phone was the dining-room chair which had collapsed under Rory one year while he was putting up Christmas decorations. The offending back leg had been glued very visibly across the break, but it was still considered too dangerous to sit on, and relegated to the hall. There was no question of its expulsion to a junk shop or similar destination, in spite of the fact that it had been acknowledged as unfit for the purpose for which chairs are designed.

"Dad," she called out twice, before hearing a distant "Hello," from upstairs.

"He's trying to find his black tie. He put it out yesterday and I must have tidied it away." She gave a guilty shudder. "I'm so glad you've come home today — I know how busy you are."

"He must be heartbroken — Dad," Charlotte ventured. She was not sure whether her mother particularly wanted to talk about Uncle John, but she did not want them to bottle anything up for her sake.

"He never cries. He just goes all white and drained looking. When he got the phone call, he came and told me and comforted me for a while, because I cry all the time — you know me — and then went out for a walk in the rain. He was gone over two hours and when he came back he was soaked right through to his underpants. He said he had been sitting on one of the swings in the park, thinking."

"Oh, poor Dad," wailed Charlotte, a tight feeling gripping her throat. She imagined him sitting hunched on one of the swings in the pouring rain, water trickling down his face, kids abandoning their football game, running past yelling to each other, a stray dog trotting over and sniffing his leg, oblivious to his distress. It was unbearable.

Her mother had slipped into the kitchen and was rummaging around in the cutlery drawer. Charlotte wandered into the living room. A vase of tall-stemmed roses was surrounded by fallen petals. She scooped them up and dropped them into a blue china urn of pot-pourri. A pair of squirrels were playing chase along the fence and round the apple tree whose branches extended into the neighbours' garden. There was a half-open letter on the table. She recognised Rory's impatient scrawl, and opened it.

> Dear all,
>   Sorry to hear about U.J. It's really sad isn't it. He was always such a laugh. I hope you are looking after yourselves. Whoever goes to the funeral, give my love to Grandma and say I'll write soon when I get the time . . .

Then there was a paragraph about his cricket team's recent performance, including dozens of names of fellow students, which Charlotte felt would probably mean as little to her parents as it did to her. He signed off, *Yours Rory*, never *love* or *love from*. She noticed that there was no question of him interrupting the cricket season to come home from Warwick for the day to see their parents. This annoyed her. She heard her father come padding into the kitchen. Going to the doorway, she saw him standing at the table in his suit and grey socks, polishing a pair of old black shoes. His wife had her back to him and was wrapping a chicken leg in aluminium foil. There was a little pile of cheese sandwiches beside her, which she chopped into four tiny quarters as if for a bridge party and squashed into a plastic box, along with the chicken leg and a tomato. They were wearing sad, distant expressions, and seemed to be suppressing sighs. This was how she saw them, framed in the doorway — her father polishing his shoes to go to his brother's funeral, and her mother making him some lunch to eat on the train. She stood there, riveted, until her father caught sight of her, dropped the shoe and the black smeared rag, and gave her an uncharacteristically fierce hug.

Charlotte drove him to the station while her mother waved them off from the doorstep and retired indoors to make a cup of coffee ready for her return.

"Thank you for coming home today, sweetie," was all Mr Rowley said on the short journey; then, as she pulled over outside the station, "We love you very much," in a strangulated voice, and he grabbed his lunch box and bolted out of the car. Charlotte drove home, the windscreen a swaying blur of tears. Later she thought it must have been a miracle she did not hit anything; barely able to see, lurching over the cross-roads without stopping, and turning the wrong way into a one-way street. 'Parents,' she thought, making the gear box snarl as she groped to find reverse. 'Just when you begin to think you can do without them, they suddenly realise they can't do without you.' Her foot slipped off the clutch, making the car leap backwards and stall. Despite repeated attempts, it would not start but each time chugged lethargically for a few seconds and then died. She redoubled her sobs. Being ambushed by a sense of her parents' dignity, and her own unworthiness, had made her weep, but being stuck behind the wheel of a recalcitrant vehicle facing the wrong way up a one-way street made her positively howl. She allowed the car to roll backwards into the kerb, so that the queue of impatient motorists who had been drumming their fingers on their steering wheels could pass.

By the time she reached home she had calmed down, and Mrs Rowley was once more out on the doorstep, this time polishing the door knob. Her father seemed to have taken the sombre mood, which had oppressed Charlotte on her arrival, with him to Aberystwyth. The house seemed brighter, warmer, and there was a smell of biscuits baking in the oven. It was as if Mr Rowley had voluntarily taken the despondency of the entire household upon his shoulders and carted it off to the funeral where it belonged.

For the first time Charlotte found it touching rather than exasperating that her mother had bothered to make biscuits especially for her, and she ate three while the chocolate was still warm and molten. Formerly she had always taken meal times to be a battleground where some terrible power struggle was being conducted for custody of her body. Her mother represented the enemy, bombarding her with heavy artillery in the form of cream buns and extra potatoes, and all Charlotte had had in the way of defence was a will of jelly and general teenage malice. There had been one period, when she was fifteen, when she had refused to eat evening meals with the family at all, claiming she was not hungry. By nine o'clock she could usually be found scraping the congealed left-overs out of the pan, or consuming vast wedges of bread and peanut butter. It had nothing to do with slimming, Charlotte now realised. It had been an act of pure self-assertion, absenting herself quite deliberately from the realm of maternal care.

Today, uncharacteristically, she found her mother's incessant nurturing a luxury rather than a burden. They sat in the living room, chatting until lunchtime, when Mrs Rowley produced a hot asparagus quiche and some grilled tomatoes. "I *am* enjoying myself," her mother said, as they divided the last slice between them, which struck Charlotte as a strange thing to say on the day of a funeral. Such was the strength of parental love that Charlotte's presence could even sweeten the bitterness of bereavement. For the first time Charlotte felt the power and the privilege of her position, and made a silent promise not to abuse it.

In the afternoon they looked through some old photo albums — there she was as a baby, not a particularly attractive one; too fat and with enormous ears. There she was again, in her father's arms, her mother looking on mistily. Motherhood. It was not for her, the life of selfless devotion to the demands, whims and outrages of the next generation. She much preferred being a daughter. But although she knew, without any doubt, that she did not want to live a replica of her mother's life, the sight of her packing a little lunch for her husband to take to a funeral had erased all trace of the scorn Charlotte had once felt for her mother's status.

When it finally came for her to leave, and she was presented with an iced fruit cake in a Huntley & Palmer's biscuit tin, she astonished her mother by dissolving uncontrollably into tears.

12

CHARLOTTE, it appeared, was not the only one who was having a memorable day. Patrick, sitting on one end of an otherwise empty seesaw in the park, was beginning to realise that things could not go on as they were. He had spent most of the afternoon taking an emotional drubbing from various quarters. Most importantly, he had had to face some unpleasant home-truths from his tutor about his chances of finishing his doctorate. He bobbed hopelessly up and down on his end of the seesaw, as if hoping some invisible force would suddenly set the machine in motion. He saw his tutor's large fleshy hand holding up a piece of work and flicking it dismissively with a finger.

"You've produced nothing longer than two thousand words all year," he said, laying the papers on his desk and looking squarely at Patrick. "Your idea is a good one, but you simply haven't come up with the work. What's gone wrong?" Dr Beamish's tiny, pale eyes peered at him from an expanse of pink bloated skin. He sat sprawled across the sofa with his legs apart, one hand smoothing wisps of hair back over his bald patch, the other stroking one of his chins expectantly. Patrick stared at the cream crocodile-skin shoes protruding from Dr Beamish's navy trousers. He took in the tight white shirt and red cravat, before finally meeting his eye.

"I don't know," he said unhelpfully. How could he tell this man, who had an intimidating army of his own publications ranked in glass cabinets behind him, that lately he had fallen victim to a form of mental paralysis: indolence. Every morning the realisation that he would have to drag himself back to his books stole over Patrick like a chilly draught. It was not that he disliked the work when he was doing it; on the contrary, he actually enjoyed it, and a whole day could pass without him once looking at his watch or breaking his concentration. He merely found it difficult, almost impossible in fact, to make that single decisive move towards his desk. He would take an unreasonable amount of time to dress, and deliberately make himself a long and elaborate breakfast — squeezing oranges when there was already a carton of juice open in the fridge, and grilling bacon and mushrooms. Then he would wash up, slowly dry the few dishes, and read the newspaper. It was farcical. He knew exactly what he was doing — deferring for as long as possible the moment when he would have to open his books and start work. It was not laziness, he was sure of that. He never sat around aimlessly with nothing to do. On the contrary, he would invent hundreds of tasks that needed to be done, urgently, at that precise moment. There was always washing to be taken to the laundry, a bicycle tyre to be pumped up, a bin to be emptied. Sometimes this process might last until twelve when he would be back into the routine of preparing lunch, and the whole cycle would start all over again. He could not say this to Dr Beamish. He could imagine only too well the contemptuous reception such an admission would receive from someone who produced a new book every year without fail. So he said nothing more illuminating than, "I don't know."

The prolific author sighed, and rolled himself round the sofa into a more comfortable position.

"Well, if you haven't brought me a mini-thesis of six thousand words by the end of term, I'm afraid I won't be able to recommend that you continue your doctorate."

Patrick nodded slowly. He liked Dr Beamish, although his dapper clothes and habit of lolling on the sofa in extravagant postures dismayed Patrick a little. It was only because Patrick was his favourite that Dr Beamish had allowed him to get this far without reproof. But his popularity seemed to have run out and now, he thought ironically, when he needed a lifeline all he was being offered was a deadline.

They exchanged some amiable conversation about a new biography of Sartre, until a knock at the door announced the arrival of the next tutee. Patrick, making no promises to complete the required piece, slipped out and trudged downstairs to the basement, intending to persuade Tyrone to come out for a walk.

DO NOT DISTURB THE DISTURBED said a sign on Tyrone's door. Patrick ignored it and knocked.

"Yeah," said a muffled voice.

Tyrone was sitting on the floor with a frying pan on his lap, eating baked beans with a dart. In the wash basin in the corner was a teetering pile of dirty plates, mugs and cutlery.

Patrick looked at him in amazement.

"I've used all my forks," said Tyrone, waving the dart in the direction of the sink. "Haven't got time to wash up. Will you test me?" He handed Patrick, who had squatted down on the floor, a wad of papers smothered in barely legible quotes.

"All right. If you'll come for a walk after that."

Tyrone shrugged non-committally.

"'Sweet is the lore ...'" began Patrick.

"er ... which nature brings ... er ... our meddling intellect ... dissects ... no, that's not right ... er, mistakes the ... oh shit."

"'Mis-shapes the beauteous forms of things / We murder to dissect.'"

"Yes, yes, I knew that," Tyrone agreed, and bulldozed his way through another three pages of Wordsworth, until he finally snatched the sheets back from Patrick in frustration.

"You don't know any of these," Patrick remonstrated, half-laughing.

"Do Milton then. I know all those."

"If you're sure you know them, there's no point in me testing you."

Tyrone jumped to his feet and balanced the frying pan on the fragile structure in the sink. He struggled into a pair of tatty grey plimsolls without unlacing them. "Right, let's go for this walk then."

Patrick recounted his conversation with Dr Beamish as they headed past the Radcliffe Camera. The wind was blowing in strong gusts, whipping at their clothes and sending dust and litter whirling along the street. A sheet of newspaper wrapped itself around Tyrone's legs, making him stumble and reach out for Patrick who had gone on ahead. They walked aimlessly along Queen Street, arms folded against the wind, heads down. Patrick had no particular destination in mind, though he frequently ended up in Rita's café in the market. It was pleasantly crowded and noisy in there and at lunchtimes Patrick inevitably found himself sharing a table with strangers, the only vestige of privacy being provided by the clouds of cigarette smoke. It was an eavesdropper's paradise; packed so closely together on unsteady classroom chairs, people tended to abandon discretion as a lost cause, and become quite theatrical in their disclosures. Patrick was silently calculating whether he could afford to buy Tyrone tea at Rita's when he noticed Alison, only a few paces away, emerging from a jeweller's shop, gazing intently at her left hand. They stopped in front of her, making her jump.

"Hello," she said, blushing as if caught out, and putting her hands behind her back casually. "Where are you off to?"

The men looked at each other. "Not sure," said Tyrone. "I was following him. What were you doing in there? Buying a ring?"

Her expression of undisguised amazement showed Tyrone that, quite unexpectedly, he had hit on the truth. He seized her left hand.

"You're engaged! Bloody hell. Why didn't you tell us?" and he gave her an unusually uninhibited hug. She could not quite bring herself to meet Patrick's eye, as he gave her a brotherly kiss on the cheek; instead she looked down at the solitaire diamond on her fourth finger. She had just collected it from the jeweller's where it had been enlarged.

"When are you getting married?" Tyrone was saying.

This seemed to throw Alison. "I don't know, to be honest. Next year sometime." She looked almost apologetic as she shrugged and made her way back to the library.

"All the world loves a lover," quoted Tyrone.

'Maybe,' thought Patrick, to whom this news had come as the second blow of the day, 'but when it's someone else's lover you love . . .' He did not feel like going to Rita's now. He would be sure to be sandwiched between ranks of amorous couples with dilated pupils, practising the sort of body language beloved of anthropologists, across their cracked-wheat salads.

Across the road, a sign advertising St Mary's church tower blew over with a bang, making them jump. It suddenly struck Patrick that he had never been up the tower, and that it would be a novel form of escape. Rather than running away, he would go up. That was what he needed — a new vantage point.

"Let's go up the tower," he said to Tyrone, and quite forgetting that his friend had a problem with heights, he dived through the traffic. He was so delighted with his idea that he barely bothered to look over his shoulder to check that Tyrone was following him. The staircase was disappointingly sturdy and modern. He had imagined a dank, chilly climb through curtains of cobwebs, until his emergence into the bright sunlight on the parapet would blind him with sudden inspiration. The broad staircase gave way at the top to one of steeply curving stone. There was only room for one-way traffic. The steps rose so sharply that Patrick, who was in front, was worried that at any moment he might find his head being used as a stair. This was more like it, he thought. The road to visionary experience ought to be difficult. The platform which surrounded all four sides of the tower was only a couple of feet across, protected by a wide stone parapet which reached chest height. Patrick leant over it, balancing on his lower arms. Oxford lay spread out before him; oblongs of green enclosed on all sides by the tall, spiky college buildings; the river making its serpentine way past fields and houses towards London and the open sea. He walked right round the tower, occasionally squashing himself against the back wall to let someone squeeze past. Queen Street was jammed with cars and buses. Groups of cyclists wove in and out of the traffic, dodging on to the pavement to avoid red lights, flowing around stationary vehicles like shoals of multi-coloured fish. It was the rush hour. Pedestrians, like tiny tinted insects, were hurrying along towards bus stops, shops and restaurants. Queues were forming beside cash machines. The Radcliffe Camera was disgorging students on to the grass. Everyone except him seemed to be moving with a sense of purpose. Tyrone joined him, keeping close to the back wall. The platform was beginning to fill up. A man with an enormous, pendulous stomach passed Patrick, holding his arms at shoulder height like someone wading out to sea. Discomfited at the difficulty he was having, he pushed rudely past Tyrone, pressing him hard against the parapet, forcing him to look over. The pavement, far below, heaved and swam. Tyrone gave a strangulated cry. Patrick looked at him in alarm, and grabbed his arm as the fat man finally eased his way past.

"Don't worry. You can't fall. I won't let you go." Tyrone's fear grew to hysteria at these words. "You would. You would," he cried wildly, tearing himself away from Patrick's grasp and staggering towards the staircase. A queue of people were coming up one after another. There was no escape.

"Calm down," Patrick tried to say, hating to be made a spectacle of, as the newcomers edged past them. Tyrone was sweating profusely, taking shallow gasping breaths, which turned into a horrifically comical snorting noise as he slumped to the floor. The tour party, still filing through the doorway, were forced to step over him. Eventually the last of them came through, giving Patrick a puzzled look as he pulled Tyrone to his feet.

"Sorry, sorry. I'm really sorry," Tyrone kept saying, as Patrick led him down the stairs. "It was just . . . you know . . ." He was having trouble articulating, and Patrick, who found public displays of emotion deeply embarrassing, was happy to cut him off with a reassuring "Don't worry," and leave it at that.

Back on the pavement, Tyrone made a titanic effort to look composed, and the two men parted, relief on both sides.

Patrick then made his way to the park behind his house, and it was there, on the seesaw, that he contemplated the depressing events of the day.

He moved on to the roundabout as the first spots of rain began to fall, turning it gently with one foot, watching the park rotate around him. The view from the tower had put things in perspective – Oxford from above was a place of walls and enclosures. For the first time, Patrick admitted to himself the extent to which he had used the college as a sanctuary, a means of deferring his expulsion into the unwelcoming world beyond. He had become directionless, ambling along with his doctorate for no better reason than that to stop required a conscious act of will. He considered his studies. Why was he doing it? Once, he vaguely recalled there had been a sense of intellectual excitement. Research had seemed as potent as alchemy in those days, promising revelations of heart-stopping significance. There must have been a precise moment when he had lost this feeling, but appropriately he could not remember it. It ought to have been a memorable moment – being brought down by disillusionment in a flying tackle – but instead it had crept up on him silently and fatally, like old age. He knew he could not continue with it now that the only remaining incentive was the desire to be called Doctor. He felt he was on the brink of making a decision. Briefly cheered by this novelty, Patrick jumped off the roundabout and walked at a brisk and optimistic pace to the house.

Having no communal sitting-room, Patrick and his four flatmates tended not to see a great deal of one another, and kept their relationships on a largely epistolary footing. There were usually demands for electricity money, notes of apology tacked to the kitchen table next to last night's dirty dishes,

IOUs choking up the money-box under the pay phone. The vinyl notice board above it was a montage of primitive doodles, shorthand and abbreviations.

A message on the kitchen door saying WILL CLEAR UP LATER was as ominous as the smell of old bacon fat and burnt toast which hung suspended in the basement stairwell as if too heavy to mount the stairs.

Patrick pushed open the door tentatively and went in. Yesterday's paper was strewn around the floor, which to his disgust felt sticky underfoot. The bin was overflowing with yoghurt pots, egg cartons and crisp wrappers. There was a red streak on the wall above it where someone had lobbed a not quite empty tin of tomatoes on to the pile. The grill pan, coated with spotty lard, had been left on the table and had fused to the plastic tablecloth. He approached the fridge, pasta shells crunching beneath his feet. Inside were nine half-eaten tins of baked beans and condensed soup in various stages of putrefaction, and a piece of chicken which had defrosted and bled all over the shelf below.

Feeling sick, Patrick wiped a coffee ring off one of the chairs with a tea-towel and sat down. Just behind a greasy plate with an apple core and a tissue stuck to it, was the radio. Absent-mindedly he turned it on. The disc-jockey thanked someone called Amanda for her comments, wished her a good evening, and invited other listeners to add their comments. There was some synthesised music, and a sound of breaking glass, before an electronic voice announced the phone number.

It was then that he heard it, sitting on a kitchen chair in the half light, amongst the filthy debris of litter and rotting food. Patrick's Song. It had been given a jazzed-up orchestral arrangement and effectively drained of all trace of emotion, but it was quite recognisable all the same. Over the music, a young female voice was extolling the merits of a new spray-on stain remover. *'Blitz' instantly dissolves stubborn marks like ink, blood and grime. Ideal for clothes and upholstery*, she gushed, as the tune jangled away in the background. 'Oh God.' Patrick put his head in his hands. The competition. He had turned Boris's treasured composition, his private gesture of friendship, into an advertiser's jingle. This was not just plagiarism, it was sacrilege. He sat there for the next hour alone, as the light faded leaving him in shadowy darkness. Then, as if the diabolical rendition of the song that had been a gift to him from Boris had provided the necessary jolt to the see-saw, he leapt to his feet, and took the stairs three at a time.

Half an hour later when he had packed his belongings into boxes, stacked them on the bed, and written cheques for remaining rent and bills, he left the house, the rain still pouring down, carrying nothing but his toothbrush, flute and a change of clothing.

13

ALISON'S meeting with Patrick and Tyrone had left her in a depressed and uneasy mood. She was furious with herself for having tried to hide her engagement ring. After all, an engagement was supposed to be a public declaration. It had not exactly taken that form in her guilty half-intoxicated acceptance in Oliver's bedroom, and this worried her. In fact, as she walked back to Salisbury Street watching other students struggling along on rusty bicycles, or walking in groups all chattering loudly over one another, she felt, merely on account of this tiny ring, excluded and alienated. Until Tyrone had questioned her, the idea of marriage as a rapid and inevitable consequence of engagement had not even occurred to her. She felt that complying with Oliver's unexpected proposal the night before had been the least she could have done, in view of her evening of unconfessed truancy. Now, as she pushed the front door open and stepped over a pile of free newspapers and junk mail, she was beginning to realise that accepting Oliver's ring was not just an isolated gesture. It had set something in motion. Causality was a word she used often enough in her essays, but never applied to reality. Alison was more used to taking the role of a bystander in her life than that of leading lady. Things just seemed to happen fortuitously, without her own intervention. This explained her hesitancy in fixing on any sort of employment or further education — she vaguely imagined bowling into some post-graduate work if she got a First, which Mrs Summers had hinted was a genuine possibility, but the idea of grappling head on with the future and forcing it to do her bidding, was a new and alarming concept.

'Why am I dissatisfied?' she asked herself, looking at her thin, tidy reflection in the huge tarnished mirror in the hall. She dropped her handbag into the rocking chair which obediently creaked into life. The newly engaged were meant to be euphoric. What was wrong with her? She supposed it had something to do with a discovery she had made only that morning.

She had been working in the spare room as usual, at the unsteady collapsible desk which shuddered as she wrote (Oliver did not like anyone using his study in case they moved anything), when after three hours of intense concentration and furious scribbling, three timed essays on the Renaissance complete, her hand, brain and bottom had become too numb to continue. There was one particular word which was troubling her, and her thesaurus seemed to have disappeared. *Chimera*. She would have to resort to Oliver's dictionary. Ignoring his injunction not to go rummaging around in his study and disturbing his papers, she pushed the door open and switched the overhead light on. The bulb was far too dim and made the room look sleazy and disreputable. She threw open the curtains, which for some reason Oliver always kept closed, and removed her calculator which she had been missing for weeks from the window sill.

Remembering that the first volume of the *Compact Oxford* had been one of the casualties of his divorce, she began to hunt around for an alternative. There was a book-case full of dictionaries beside his desk. She had never seen so many. Dictionaries of proverbs, Latin phrases, French, Italian, Greek, Classical mythology, Biblical terms, Opera, Middle English, Difficult words. She picked up this last one and opened it with interest.

'FLAUNT/FLOUT. These words have very different meanings

and *must not* be confused. . .' Alison was intrigued. She had always used the two words interchangeably and people had never had any trouble understanding her. This was a new experience, being ticked off by a book. She flicked through it further.

'UNINTERESTED / DISINTERESTED.' Again she felt chastened. 'These words are not synonyms,' the type positively barked at her. ' "Disinterested" should *only* be used where the sense is "unprejudiced" or "unbiased".'

Quite forgetting what she had originally been looking for, Alison continued to browse around the room, fascinated. Oliver was so secretive about his writing, and so protective about the sanctity of his study, that she had only been in there a few times since she had moved in, to take him cups of coffee or call him to the telephone. Lately he had grown more and more reticent about *The Last Days of the Critic*. A year ago when she had been nothing more to him than a pupil, he had been delighted with her interest, and frequently used her as a sounding board for ideas. Recently, although he still spent as much time in the dusty gloom of his study as ever, he was evasive about his progress.

"You can read it when it's finished," he would say, kissing her on the forehead. "I don't want any criticism until then, in case it puts me off my stride." This was reasonable enough, but time was passing and he still gave no hint of a likely completion date. Consumed by curiosity, Alison decided to have a quick glance at the manuscript. Perhaps he had finished it and was waiting for her to pass her exams before announcing a double celebration. She had to know. The desk was littered with papers which she tried to read without rearranging them. None of them had anything to do with literature. One was a letter to the tax office, there were several bank statements, invitations to lecture at summer schools, and rejection slips from various journals. She opened the top drawer. Inside was a manila envelope file marked LAST DAYS OF THE CRITIC – MANUSCRIPT AND NOTES. She picked it up, feeling its heaviness with mounting excitement. It must be nearly finished, she thought, as she sat down in one of the slumping armchairs. The file contained only a thick pad of paper, which was blank apart from a six-page introduction, five pages of notes, a bibliography and unconnected jottings. This was the product of years of laborious research? The entire yield of countless hours in retreat? Disbelief and dismay making her heart race, she read through the introduction, hoping desperately to find traces of the wit and originality which had marked his first publication. 'After all, *The Last Days of the Novel* was a classic in its day,' she said to herself, unwittingly condemning it to instant obsolescence. But the more she read, the more it made her squirm, with its archness and false modesty.

She had put it back exactly as she had found it, and tried to rationalise her discomfort away, but from that moment she felt as though a precious part of their relationship had been cancelled out. She would not be able to confront Oliver about it, because that would involve an admission of her own duplicity. Instead, she would be punished for her curiosity by having to keep it to herself.

Taking off her coat, and hanging it on the banisters in an unconscious act of defiance, Alison was about to go into the kitchen and make a sandwich, when she heard a noise upstairs. She stiffened, holding her breath. It sounded like faint laughter; coughing, perhaps. Oliver was at a lecture. Beckford was lolling in his basket. This reassured her. He usually brought the house down if a stranger so much as rang the doorbell. Alison crept up the first flight of stairs.

"Hello," she croaked into the air, helplessly. There was a sound of scuffling which seemed to be coming from the attic. 'Rats?' she wondered, then flushed hot and cold as she remembered the laughing. She stepped into the bedroom looking for a suitable weapon. That was the trouble with Oliver — he never left anything lying around. She picked up a can of hairspray and crept up to the top landing. The trap door was hanging open and a step ladder was positioned beneath it.

"Who's there?" she called out, her voice squeaking. She aimed the aerosol can towards the black hole in the ceiling.

"Hello. Don't be frightened. I'm Oliver's ex-wife," said a familiar voice, and the bright red face of Rosie Floyd, surrounded by a halo of ginger hair, peered out of the attic. The two women looked at each other's astonished faces for a couple of seconds.

"Oh Lord," said Rosie. "I never dreamt you were . . ." and then relapsed into silence.

"I didn't realise . . ." Alison said simultaneously. Rosie climbed down the ladder, a black dustbin bag in one hand.

"I just came back to pick up some things which I've been missing for ages. I knew he'd have put them in the attic. Naughty of me to use the key, I suppose."

Alison was still slightly dazed. Looking down, she became aware that she had her finger on the spray button, pointed towards Rosie.

"What were you going to do with that? Glue me to death?" the intruder laughed.

"Cup of tea?" said Alison weakly. Wasn't that what women always resorted to in a crisis? At the back of her mind various problems were churning around, failing to resolve themselves. Was Rosie really the same person as Rosalind, the schizo-phrenic gorgon, the emotionally crippled man-hater of Oliver's accounts. How could her own fiancé be the infantile chauvinist, the monster of emotional and intellectual medio-crity described by Rosie. It was a nightmare. Neither account fitted her image, but of the two . . .

"You haven't seen a pair of tasselled cowboy boots anywhere?" Rosie was saying, poking around in the coat cupboard. "I haven't seen them since I left. They must be somewhere."

Alison poured boiling water into the teapot and prodded disconsolately at the teabags, trying to submerge them, but they kept bobbing back up again. Her mind was whirling like a mouse on a wheel, getting nowhere. Did not her relationship with Oliver depend for its existence on their mutual contempt for his first wife, and everything she represented? Had not Oliver fostered her sense of rivalry with the unknown woman, during the first few months, by comparing Alison's every action either favourably or unfavourably with the errant original? The discovery that this suburban Goneril was an acquaintance whom she admired and even tried to emulate, had wrenched the carpet of blind prejudice from under her feet with unexpected violence.

She felt as though Oliver had deliberately, systematically, tricked her, playing on her insecurity in order to manipulate her into the sort of companion he wanted. He had only to say the words "Rosalind used to do such and such," to see her instantly doing the opposite. "I've been through this argument before," would reduce her to a flushed and humiliated silence. "Rosalind always spent hours on the phone," led to the receiver being slammed down on any unfortunate caller as soon as Alison heard the click of the gate.

She could hardly concentrate on Rosie's chatter. Memories of Oliver's iniquitous behaviour kept accosting her.

"Oh, I'd forgotten this," Rosie was saying, pointing at a marquetry inlaid violin, which stood on a glass shelf out of reach. It was Oliver's most treasured possession. "Credit where it's due — he did it all himself, you know," Rosie continued, nodding.

"I know," Alison answered glumly. "He won't even let me touch it in case I break it. No, that's not quite true. He did once let me run my finger over it under supervision, to feel how well it had been finished ..." She trailed off.

"There's no doubt about it, he has many admirable qualities — a lot of delightful little ways, really. And he's probably mellowed since I knew him ..." The insincerity in her tone was palpable. Rosie was clearly trying to compensate for the slanderous comments she had inadvertently made about Oliver in the past, thought Alison. She put her hands behind her back and eased off her engagement ring. She would spare Rosie the embarrassment of having to congratulate her. Once again she was besieged by a sense of treachery. She had only been engaged a day and already she had twice tried to hide the evidence. Any moment she expected to hear a cock crow.

115

Rosie stood up to leave. "I don't want him to catch me here," she said, picking up her coat and the dustbin bag, and giving Alison an unexpected kiss on the cheek. The door banged shut behind her and Alison was left alone. It was ironic. If Rosie had tried to denigrate or belittle Oliver, Alison would immediately have leapt to his defence, but her desperate groping towards compliments had only revealed their woeful inaccuracy. Was delightful really the right word to describe Oliver's ways? She thought not. Volatile was more like it. Mellow wouldn't quite do either. Alison was in the middle of composing a mental list of his attributes under the headings FOR and AGAINST, when the scrutinee himself walked in. She had had no trouble with the against column and was faltering at intelligent, generous and faithful on the plus side, when his arrival spared her further leaps of the imagination. He dropped his briefcase uncharacteristically and threw his coat over the back of a chair.

"Rosalind's been here," he said accusingly, in a tone that was half-way between a question and a statement. "I saw the car driving away from the house. Did you meet her?" He sounded upset and rattled.

"Yes," Alison answered, looking him straight in the eye.

"I suppose she has been telling you all sorts of terrible things about me," he said gloomily, sinking into a chair.

"No, on the contrary—"

"What was she doing here anyway?" he interrupted. "She's got no right to come in uninvited, the bitch."

Alison winced as she remembered how it used to give her a thrill of triumph to hear him abuse her. Now it sounded ugly and distasteful.

"She didn't stay long. But Oliver, I knew her already. She's the one who has been looking after my tramp. I only found out today that she was your wife."

He looked at her in amazement, a frown of disbelief crumpling his forehead. "I don't believe it. You must have spent more time in the last few weeks with my ex-wife than you have with me."

"Don't be ridiculous." Alison did some quick calculations

to confirm her assumption that he was wildly exaggerating.

"Well, I don't want you going round there again," he replied brusquely, as though that settled it, and he stood up and went to hang his coat in the cloakroom, as if to signal the end of the discussion.

"Wait a minute!" Alison called indignantly after him. "You can't tell me who I can or can't visit. I happen to quite like her." He looked at her, sensing rebellion.

"I knew you would take her side against me." He strode back into the room, too agitated to sit down. "That is precisely what she would want. She won't rest until she's driven a wedge between us."

"You're being para—" Alison began, but before she could finish her sentence, Oliver had snatched the words half-formed from her mouth.

"Paranoid?" He pummelled it for a while before sending it back. "Paranoid! That's exactly the sort of patronising remark Rosalind would make to try and undermine me."

"Don't keep comparing us," Alison screamed. "I'm sick of it. I sometimes think you are trying to mould me into her image, just so you can say 'I told you so.'"

"That's crap. Why would I want to go through that misery for a second time? You've no idea what it's like, divorce."

"I should do by now," she replied viciously. "I hear about it often enough."

They had both forgotten what the original argument was about by now. Neither could remember what it was they were trying to prove. It had merely become an exercise in malice to see whose insults had the more fatal sting.

"There's a really nasty side to you," Oliver spat, pacing up and down the room, while Alison cringed against the wall. "And don't flinch away as if you're afraid I'm going to hit you," his anger increasing by the second. "You know I've never touched you, but you love to make me out to be a tyrant, just like she did."

"You are." Alison stepped forward, her face pinched with contempt for him and despair for herself. "Mentally. You resent any of my achievements, and you never stop trying

117

to break my spirit with your endless comparisons. I know what sort of woman you want — and she doesn't exist. One with the looks of a film star, the brain of a professor and the ambition of a charlady."

"That's a lie. I've shown nothing but consideration for you while you've been studying. But you — you treat me as if I'm your father or something. Someone to pay the bills and provide the security and give you lifts. Someone who can be left behind while you go out enjoying yourself. Someone whose sexual advances have to be repulsed."

She gave a whimper, as they stood glaring at each other. She should have known this would be a fight to the death. For Oliver, to be right was always more important than to be happy. Alison found she was squinting, as if the harsh light of home-truths hurt her eyes. After a few seconds Oliver looked away.

"I'm going to my study to work," he said in a quiet but menacing voice.

Before she could stop herself, a "hah" of derision escaped her. She instantly regretted it. He looked up sharply and in that fraction of a second took in her expression and everything it meant. She knew, and he knew she knew, the emptiness at the core of him, and as they held each other's gaze she felt as though she was poised on the edge of a yawning abyss.

He gave her a look of pure, undiluted hatred, turned on his heel and left, banging the living-room door. A moment late she heard him thundering away at the grand piano, beating out Tchaikovsky's first piano concerto at full volume, making the window panes rattle, while Beckford howled mournfully in the background.

She felt sorry for the things she had said, but knew that no amount of remorse or contrition could unsay them. They may as well have carved the words into each other's flesh with a sharp knife. Covering up the wounds now would simply make them fester and spread. She crept upstairs, shaking, and threw her books and a few clothes back in the suitcase. The music was still reverberating around the house

118

with punishing insistence. 'I don't know why he doesn't simply nail the loud pedal to the floor,' she thought spitefully. She tiptoed into the living room for a last look around. On the floor beneath the glass shelf, the marquetry violin lay smashed to pieces, the pegs broken and the strings unnaturally slackened over the fingerboard. The smooth varnished body had been shattered into ugly splinters. It had clearly been dislodged from its rest by the vibrations of the piano next door, but it seemed to Alison that their argument had released a destructive kinetic energy into the room which had had to spend itself in violence and chaos.

Still shaking, she picked up her suitcase and pushed open the door to Oliver's room; the sound of crashing piano keys suddenly amplified. He did not stop playing. He did not even look up.

"Oliver," she said, over the din. He ignored her. "I'm going now. For good."

He still made no reply, and no acknowledgement, but kept belabouring the keyboard, pumping at the pedal with his foot. She put her door key deliberately on top of the piano, put her coat on and walked out, still dazed, bewildered by the suddenness of the rupture. Half-expecting Oliver to come running after her, pleading and crying, she set off towards College, pushing her bicycle along the pavement with one hand and holding her case with the other. The sky was dark and rumbling and a few large splashes of rain left dark spots on her coat. It was difficult to control the bicycle one-handed, and it kept swerving into her, scraping its pedal against her ankle. The dizzy shiveriness she had taken to be a combination of rage and anxiety had not left her, and as she turned into the main road, she became aware that she had a raging headache. She looked behind her; no one was following. Leaning the bicycle against a wall, she balanced the suitcase precariously across the basket and started again.

A flash of sheet lightning lit up the Woodstock Road in vivid black and white, there was an ominous grumble, and the rain began to come down in torrents. She quickened her pace, but realising that she was going to get soaked anyway,

119

slowed down again. Her tights were splattered with muddy water, and torn where she had caught her leg against the pedals. Her make-up had started to run too. She could feel a greasy film of foundation sliding down her cheeks. Through the blur of the rain, the sky looked oppressively low and dark, although it was only early evening. She felt as though she was hallucinating. Someone hurrying past with a newspaper on his head shouted, "Hello, Alison," but she did not recognise him or have the presence of mind to do anything but plod onwards. By the time she reached the college, she was chilled to the bone. Her fingers were too numb to cope with the bicycle lock, so she left it propped against the railings. As soon as she turned her back, it slipped over with a crash, but she ignored it and didn't turn back.

There was a letter for her on the notice board, and another stuffed under her door. She held them both between her chattering teeth while she stripped off her wet clothes and dragged on a pair of pyjamas. She dropped a couple of painkillers into a glass of water and watched them disintegrate, before climbing into bed. It had been made up with stiff white sheets, and she pulled them around her gratefully, her convulsive shivers making the bed creak and shudder against the wall.

She tore open the first envelope. It was from Rosie.

> Dear Alison,
> I hope I didn't get you into trouble. Bad news, I'm afraid. Archie never made his gardening job today. When I got back from Oliver's I found a back window smashed and a bottle of whisky missing, and no sign of Archie. I'll leave his door open tonight in case, but I doubt if he'll come back. I am drowning my sorrows in the bottle of tonic he was kind enough to leave me. I hope he gets an evil hangover.
> Love,
> Rosie / Rosalind

Alison sighed. Her headache had almost obliterated her ability to think. Why wasn't it going off? She looked up and realised that she had not actually drunk the aspirin. She took a swig, the scum of undissolved powder catching the back of her throat and making her splutter.

The room swam in and out of focus. With an effort she picked up the second note. It was from Patrick, and she had to read it a couple of times before she took it in properly.

> Dear Alison,
>
> This is just a short note to say goodbye for now, and good luck. I have decided to join the Brotherhood. I have been considering it for some time, but it was only today that I finally made up my mind. I am going to Wales for a while with Greg to prepare myself for taking their vows. I have sent a note to Beamish saying that I no longer want to continue my doctorate.
>
> Best wishes in your exams — and to Charlotte and Tyrone too, and for your future with Oliver. Perhaps I will see something of you when I return to Oxford?
>
> Yours,
> Patrick

So Greg had won. Her head thumped and throbbed, and the letter slipped to the floor as she sank into a fitful and delirious sleep.

14

After Tyrone and Patrick parted company at the bottom of St Mary's Tower, Tyrone turned into Radcliffe Square and sat down on the library steps to get his breath back. His heart was pounding as though it would dislodge itself from its moorings. Every so often it would miss a beat, making him inhale sharply and claw at his shirt. 'Whatever possessed me to go up that tower,' he thought. The lethargic calmness that had begun to descend since his day out with Charlotte was once more blighted by anxiety and panic. His head throbbed. He felt as though a couple of steel bolts were trying to force their way out through his eyeballs. People were emerging from the library, rubbing their eyes, lighting up cigarettes. The building, with its impressive dome, always made him think of a cathedral. It was like a place of worship inside too, with the librarian presiding in hushed tones over the reserve stack like a priestess. Even the subdued glow of the lamps seemed to have been designed to promote reverence rather than illumination. There had been vows, too, he remembered – to refrain from taking food, drink or umbrellas into the reading room, and not to wear stilettos or to kindle fires therein. It was like a bizarre religion. Adultery was in, if the habits of dons were anything to go by, but umbrellas were definitely out.

The cold stone of the steps was too uncomfortable to keep him there long. He headed back to the shops and into his favourite tobacconist where he bought a packet of cigarettes and some matches. He always forgot his lighter and was constantly buying new boxes of matches. He had hundreds in his room. Despite the fact that his usual brand were available from every newsagent and automatic dispenser (forbidden fruit machines, Patrick called them), he often went out of his way to this shop, just to look at the assortment of different packets and the racks of polished pipes. He kept intending to give up, at some unspecified date in the future, but was not convinced he really wanted to sacrifice quality of life for mere longevity.

What was that anecdote he had come across recently? Coleridge, he remembered, had for a time employed a bodyguard to eject him forcibly from apothecaries' shops whenever he tried to buy opium. A sort of vigorous external conscience. Or was it De Quincey? His mind wandered. 'Perhaps I could persuade Patrick to trail me full-time and bundle me out of tobacconists in the same way.' He lit up with some difficulty, nearly scorching his hands in an attempt to shield the flame from the wind, then turned the corner and headed down the hill towards the river.

He stopped on the bridge and looked over at the black water. Some shrieking girls in a punt were trying to push away from the side, dropping crisps into the water to attract a group of ducks. A crew was out on the river practising. The boat looked like a large ungainly centipede, thought Tyrone, as it turned through one hundred and eighty degrees, blades waving unevenly. The coach was sitting astride a bicycle on the towpath, bellowing instructions through a megaphone. The boat finally swung into the right position facing upstream, sat poised in the water for a brief second, then at a barked command from the cox slid forward and, gathering speed, sliced up the river, the blades sweeping back with apparently effortless regularity.

Moments later a crocodile of schoolchildren came weaving along the path, led by a straight-backed teacher in a tweed sports jacket, which was slightly too short in the sleeve and made his hands look unnaturally large. He gave a salute of thanks to the coach, who stood back to let them pass before jumping on his bicycle and pedalling furiously after his disappearing crew.

Tyrone crossed the bridge and walked slowly down the towpath, kicking a stone along in front of him, feeling slightly dizzy. Apart from the frying pan of baked beans, he had not eaten all day, and had now passed beyond the hunger barrier into a state of lightheadedness and nausea. The cigarettes did not help. He felt a spot of rain on his sleeve, and then another, and as he turned back to head for home and shelter, he stopped, rooted to the spot in terror at what he saw. For there on the bridge, leaning over and looking at his crumpled reflection in the rippling water, was the sandy-haired boy from the photograph.

Before Tyrone could move or call out, the figure on the bridge had straightened up and sauntered off in the direction of the High Street. Tyrone tried to shout after him but found his mouth had dried up and his voice had become a hoarse rasp. As he raced towards the bridge, there was a flash of lightning and a deafening thunderclap. For the briefest interval there was an eerie silence, and then the rain began to pour down. Oblivious to the weather, Tyrone sprinted on, and scrambled up to the road, missing the top step and crashing on to his knees, scraping one shin painfully. He got to his feet in time to see the young man disappearing through a gate into Christchurch Meadow.

'Sean,' he kept saying to himself in a trance-like daze. The sane side of him knew without any doubt that Sean lay rotting into the earth of the Cornish churchyard where as boys they used to crouch behind the gravestones for a furtive smoke. Yet, in spite of this certainty, he felt driven by an obsessive compulsion to pursue the vision on the bridge and confront it.

He reached the gateway to the meadows, puffing, gasping and vowing to give up cigarettes. To his consternation, there was no sign of his quarry. There were a couple of girls carrying lacrosse sticks, walking towards him, and a mother with three small children in the distance. Frantically he hurried on, looking towards the river and across the meadows. Just past the college building a path branched off to the left, leading into an alleyway to the High Street. At the corner a harassed-looking woman was trying to coax a golden retriever puppy to budge from the wet floor where it was crouching, its large belly and paws flattened against the ground. Each time she tugged at the lead to make it stand up, it would brace itself even more firmly, take the lead between its teeth and tug back.

Tyrone approached her breathlessly.

"You haven't seen a bloke with sandy-coloured hair and freckles, wearing a green jacket, have you?"

The woman looked up. "Yes, I think so. Youngish?" Tyrone nodded eagerly. "He went up there," and she pointed towards the High Street. Thanking her, he broke into a run, splashing carelessly through the puddles that were already forming on the muddy path. The wind was driving the rain straight into his face. He reached the gate half-way along the path, just as a group of elderly men and women arrived from the opposite direction. They seemed to be taking a lifetime to negotiate their way through.

'Come on, come on,' Tyrone was saying to himself, with mounting frustration. 'Oh please,' he thought, quelling the urge to bang his head against the railings as the last of them shuffled through an inch at a time.

He came out on to the main road, soaking wet and shuddering for breath. Each time he inhaled it felt like a stab of cold metal. He looked up and down. Although the street was not crowded, there were too many black umbrellas bobbing and swaying for him to see clearly. He had lost him.

At the entrance to the alleyway was a cash machine at which a queue of people was waiting, some with newspapers on their heads, others hunching their shoulders against the rain.

'One of them must have seen him,' he thought, tapping an elderly man on the back and clearing his throat to attract his attention. The man turned round unsteadily. It was Boris.

Tyrone was so surprised and delighted that for a crucial

moment he forgot himself and said, "Boris, did you see which direction the fair-haired bloke . . ." and then evaporated into mortified silence as he realised. Ilsa, standing behind Boris, came to his rescue.

She pointed up the High Street toward Magdalen College. "I think he went up there, Tyrone," she said evenly, in a tone which suggested that although no offence was taken, she did not feel inclined to let him off altogether.

Embarrassed and upset, Tyrone burbled a combination of thanks and apologies and ran off in the direction she had indicated. Dodging around obstructive pedestrians, cannoning into anyone who stopped without warning, he felt a mounting sense of defeat. Sean (he was mentally referring to his prey by that name now) might have disappeared into any of the colleges, side roads, or even jumped on a bus. But as he drew level with Magdalen Bridge, he saw him, hands in pockets, head down, weaving through the cars which were moving at a steady pace around the roundabout. Slithering on the greasy paving stones. Tyrone increased his pace as the young man vanished out of sight again, up the main Cowley Road.

A momentary lull in the traffic allowed Tyrone to cross without pausing to the nearby roundabout, but fear of losing Sean was making him careless. As he stepped off the kerb, a large silver car came swinging around towards him, its headlights turning the rain drops into glittering crystals. Tyrone's leg muscles instantly seized up, pinning him to the spot, as the driver, with a grimace, pumped at the brakes and brought the car to a screaming halt next to him. It was so close that Tyrone was able to put one hand on the bonnet to steady himself and to see quite clearly the furious expression of the driver, who was swearing inaudibly at him across the slicing windscreen wipers. Tyrone raised an apologetic hand and made off up the Cowley Road, as the irate motorist leapt out of the car and yelled at him across the bonnet.

"Come here, you bloody idiot," he shrieked, then turned round to vent his anger on the queue of cars which was trying to squeeze past, hooting indignantly.

Tyrone's legs were still wobbling from the fright. It occurred to him that he was not only soaked, but freezing. About one hundred yards on, the elusive figure had stopped to look in a shop window.

"Sean," Tyrone called out, slowing down to a walk. The young man looked around, as did several other pedestrians who were within earshot, but his face was obscured by shadows. Gaining in confidence, Tyrone waved a hello, but the man had already turned away and had quickened his pace.

He rehearsed what would happen when they eventually came face to face. He would grab him by the shoulders and say "Sean, you old bastard. We all thought you were dead," and Sean would look incredulous at first, and then ecstatic and say "Tyrone!" and they would hug each other fiercely. Tyrone could feel his grip on the rational slipping away, but it was such a pleasant change to feel a germ of hope stirring that he was not about to let it be crushed by mere reason.

The man had stopped outside the Women's Centre, propping himself against a wall and lighting a cigarette. He kept looking at his watch and shifting impatiently from one foot to the other.

'I've got him now,' Tyrone thought, his teeth chattering from cold and excitement. He was ten yards away now, and about to call out once more, when he suddenly stopped. A girl with long auburn hair had emerged from the Women's Centre, wrestling with a jammed umbrella, and on catching sight of her, the man had thrown down his cigarette and pulled her into his arms. They kissed each other passionately, quite without inhibition and, Tyrone noticed, with careful manoeuvres to avoid the girl's heavily pregnant belly.

As he stood there dumbly, like a man who has just caught his wife in an act of adultery, an uninvited witness to this display of tenderness, a car pulling out of the turning opposite caught the three of them in the sweep of its headlights. The couple broke apart and Tyrone could see for the first time that his quarry bore no more than a passing resemblance to Sean, and that he was staring at him over his girlfriend's head with an undisguised look of hostility. Tyrone shrank back.

"What are you staring at?" the boyfriend demanded, stepping forward threateningly. Tyrone, transfixed by dismay and shame, could not move or speak. Enraged, the man took another step towards him.

"Piss off, will you!" he exploded, breaking away from his girlfriend's restraining arm and launching himself towards Tyrone.

Tyrone fled, plunging blindly through the traffic and along the back streets, his face burning with humiliation and misery. 'I really must be going mad,' he thought. He knew Sean was dead; he had helped escort the coffin — that had been the thing that really hurt at the funeral, seeing it wheeled along on an absurd sort of collapsible shopping trolley. Yet, for a few moments, as he was pursuing the evasive figure, he had almost believed him to be a visitation, a doppelganger sent to free him from the burden of the past. He ran on, not caring where, certain only of the fact that he was the loneliest and most unlovable person in Oxford. It was dark now and the rain was pouring down mercilessly, as though it would never stop. The pavements were deserted. Tyrone was so saturated by this time that water was running off him as fast as it fell.

He never did know exactly how long he spent, aimlessly roaming the streets that evening, cold, soaked and with a relentless desperation to keep moving at all costs, but when he finally stopped outside the iron gate of the college annexe, the buildings opposite were in darkness. He dropped the key several times before getting it in the keyhole. A dark narrow alleyway led to the porch, and on the left, half-way along, was a steep flight of stairs down to the laundry. Tyrone had a recurrent fear of coming back drunk one night and falling headlong down it by mistake. He groped unsuccessfully for the light switch, then gave up. A curtained window of the college library threw out a dim light, casting barred shadows on the fence. He shut the gate with a clang, and had just locked it, when a figure loomed up from the steps, blocking the passage. It was too murky to pick him out clearly, but

Tyrone guessed from the matted hair and stale whisky fumes that it was a tramp, woken by the sound of the gate.

"Excuse me," he said politely, trying to ease past, but the tramp seized him by the arm and, putting his face unbearably close to Tyrone's, coughed warm sickly breath all over him, before saying, "You haven't got fifty pence, have you?" His words were slurred and punctuated with sniffs. Tyrone wrenched his arm free angrily.

"No, I haven't got any on me." This was true. The tramp did not budge.

"Bloody students. Rich kids," he half-snarled, half-coughed. "Give us a fag then." He lunged at Tyrone, swaying dangerously near the top of the stone steps. Filled with revulsion, Tyrone barged past him, giving him an almighty shove. He watched in horror as the tramp reeled backwards, teetered for a moment on the top step, his arms clawing the air, and plummeted down the stairs, landing with an ugly thud at the bottom. It all seemed to happen in slow motion, the look of alarm, the flailing arms, the graceless descent to the hard stone floor.

Tyrone, stupefied with panic, peered down into the stairwell, but could make out nothing more than shadows.

"Hey . . ." he pleaded. "Are you okay?"

No answer. Fumbling along the wall, he found the light switch. The tramp was lying on his back, his arms thrown out and both legs sprawled up the steps. His eyes were open and staring, and he was quite, quite dead.

In spite of this, all Tyrone could register at that moment was a distant glimmer of recognition. For a second he seemed to be looking down the years into his own future and seeing himself as an old man. For incredibly, impossibly, the dead man before him was dressed in Tyrone's old clothes.

15

IT was nearly midnight of the same day when Charlotte arrived back in Oxford. She had waited with her mother until ten, when Mr Rowley had rung from the station asking for a lift. Charlotte had picked him up and was relieved to see him looking composed, quiet, and happy to be home. He had silently slipped her a couple of ten-pound notes before they got out of the car. She had not the heart, or the conscience, to tell him that her mother had just done the same.

Mrs Rowley had turned out every pot, purse and pocket to furnish Charlotte with some cash, scrabbling in the bottom of discarded handbags for elusive pound coins.

"Don't tell your father," she said, pressing a fistful of notes and loose change into Charlotte's hand.

"I won't. I promise," Charlotte replied. They both knew the deceit to be superfluous, as Mr Rowley would be the last person to object to the handout, but they enjoyed the gesture of illicit female confederacy anyway.

She had originally intended to stay the night with her parents, but the sight of her old bedroom filled her with such a sense of sadness and alienation that she could not bear to stay. There was the earless, eyeless teddy propped against the pillow, the splodgy peach and blue door — the product of a weekend of injudicious rag-rolling — and the wallpaper, peppered with the scars of posters too hastily removed. There was her old cactus plant, sprouting with fuzzy thumbs. It was the only thing she had ever been able to keep alive. In spite of her negligence, it had managed to replicate itself endlessly until transplanting had threatened to become a full-time job. All her other plants had shrivelled and died within weeks of acquisition. Her mother had insisted that it was because lying in at the weekends with the curtains closed had starved them of light. Charlotte replied that tropical vegetation could hardly be expected to flourish in a room where ice frequently formed on the nozzle of the plant spray.

In the corner was her old bean-bag, filled not with beans but with polystyrene balls — Mrs Rowley fearing weevil infestations. The filling over the years had become more and more compressed, until anyone sitting down on it too heavily risked hitting the floor. One day, she remembered, the cover had torn and she had found herself smothered in tiny clinging white beads. They were infuriatingly perverse. The more one brushed them, the more persistently they stuck. Eventually she had had to lie on the floor while her mother ran over her with the hoover.

She had noted with amusement that the junkery, an old free-standing wardrobe, had not been tampered with in her absence. Mrs Rowley kept threatening to dispose of her arbitrary assemblage of curiosities, but somehow never quite had the resolve to carry it through. Inside were sacks of old toys; broken tennis rackets with slackened strings; jigsaw pieces spilling out of torn, floppy boxes; a frisbee, horribly misshapen from sitting overnight on a radiator; a collection of large oval shells that Uncle John had brought back from the South Pacific. ("One man's coastal debris is another man's avocado dish," he had said.) One of her favourite pieces was a necklace made from plastic imitation walnuts, which she had been given one Christmas by a great-aunt. It seemed to Charlotte the height of cynicism for a factory to be turning out plastic food while half the world went starving, and the height of self-mockery to choose the walnut, the least ornamental of objects, as an item of jewellery. In one of the boxes was an old diary of Rory's, from when he was seven. It had only been kept up until February, and yielded interesting entries like 'Went to Granny's. She didn't give me anything,' which, Charlotte felt, was a sad reflection on the state of the infantile imagination. Wordsworth would have been horrified. Then there were her own diaries, from the ages of eight to fifteen. She kept intending to consign them to the flames of the kitchen boiler, but was always overcome by sentimentality at the critical time. Most of the early volumes, however, testified to little but the paltriness of her journalistic efforts. 'Went to school', 'Went to school', 'Went to school', for the weekdays, and 'Went out', or 'Stayed in', at weekends. An intriguing section from the early teens was written entirely in code, presumably to foil the prying parental eye, but sadly took no account of the inadequacies of the adult memory, its meaning now lost to her for ever. One page in particular made her cringe. It was written in the back of the notes section — she must have been eleven at the time. 'Things I Will Never Do', the title proclaimed pompously, and beneath was a bizarre list of apparently iniquitous practices:

1 Dye my hair.
2 Smoke.
3 Have sex before marriage.
4 Drink.
5 Have my ears pierced.
6 Get myself pregnant.

Charlotte had pondered these for a moment, puzzled slightly by the curious order of preference, and by the crucial misconception of basic biology revealed in number six. All these fragments of her past filled her with such an uncanny sense of isolation, as if her room was more of a museum than a place to live, that she suddenly felt very old. Very old and very much nearer to death than to the world from which these relics dated. It was this that determined her to return to Oxford that same night, to a room which did not keep accosting her with memories.

The train brought her to Oxford station at half-past eleven, and she sat outside waiting for a taxi for a quarter of an hour before deciding to walk. The rain storm had died down by now and the air was warm and balmy. The pavements looked black and oily in the blue light of the shop windows. She walked briskly up the middle of the road, remembering stories of women being dragged into parked cars. The important thing, the self-defence tutor had told her, was not to look like a victim. Which was all very well, Charlotte thought, but you had no way of knowing what a victim looked like, unless you became one. Then you knew. She clutched her keys between her fingers like a knuckle-duster.

St Mary's clock tower was just striking twelve as she approached the college gate. As she stood there, trying to ease her key ring off her middle finger on which it was tightly wedged, there was a high-pitched wail, the door flew open and a young girl in a white gown tore out, sobbing. As soon as she saw Charlotte, who was rooted to the spot in terror, she straightened up, gave her a nod, and strolled calmly along the pavement and round the corner. Before Charlotte could do anything more than gawp after the disappearing girl, she heard an amplified voice from inside the quad saying, "Right. Thank you, everyone. Can we prepare the next scene now?" Her heartbeat gradually returning to normal, Charlotte pushed the lodge door open a fraction and squeezed through. Inside, the quad was brightly lit by floodlights mounted on metal supports, and crowds of people in shimmering costumes were milling around. In one corner there was a scaffolding tower, reaching higher than the roof of the college chapel on which a cameraman was perched like a pirate in a crow's nest.

Along one wall a table was spread with a fantastic banquet. There were several roasted birds, more like ostriches than chickens, a monstrous ham, and jugs and bowls whose contents she could not make out. There were dishes towering with fruit — grapes, plums, apples and oranges — a round pie with a glossy brown crust, and dishes of bonbons and jellies.

Charlotte watched, fascinated, hoping she would not be

hauled out of the shadows and told to clear off. The girl in the white gown had returned, and was having last-minute adjustments made to her hair. It was taken down from its braids and brushed briskly by a young woman in a blue tracksuit with a cigarette dangling from the corner of her mouth. She then replaited it into a shiny black rope, coiled it around the girl's head, and pinned it in place, finishing off with a hissing jet of hairspray which made the girl cough and cover her eyes. Just in front of Charlotte, another youngster — a boy in a white doublet and hose, his fair hair cut into an immaculate pudding basin — was pacing around, silently going through his script.

One of the actors, dressed as a clown and plucking idly at a mandolin, approached her. He must have been about six foot eight.

"You're not one of us?" he asked, strumming a chord and looking at her with concentration.

The question was superfluous. Among the forest of starched skirts and bristling ruffs, Charlotte had never looked more out of place.

"No I'm not, actually," she confessed, making a conscious effort not to address his codpiece which was almost at microphone level. "I was trying to get back to my room. May I stay and watch?"

"Not up to me. Shouldn't think anyone would even notice if you kept back here." He was wearing a pointed hat with a bell on the end, and a perilously short tunic. The crotch of his tights was sagging almost to his knees. He hauled them up.

"Impossible to get the blasted things in my size," he explained. "Can't think how you women wear them. They're so bloody itchy."

"Well, stockings are better," Charlotte admitted, "because they allow a free flow of air around the er ... thighs" (even with her contempt for euphemism she couldn't bring herself to say 'genitals' in front of a total stranger), "but then they've got all sorts of dubious bondage connotations."

"Gosh," said the clown. "It must be terrible being a woman." He sounded genuinely sympathetic.

134

Charlotte could hardly believe her luck; it was not often she was fed such a line, and she was about to reply with some withering aphorism, when the blond boy in front of her threw down his script and turned to the clown.

"All this waiting around is driving me mad," he moaned.

"What's the film?" Charlotte asked. It looked like a medieval *Wizard of Oz*.

"*Romeo and Juliet*," replied the clown. He pointed at the young boy. "Kevin's Romeo."

Kevin smiled an acknowledgement, before wandering over to the girl with braided hair and giving her plait a sly tug. Blushing with annoyance, she repositioned it demurely before turning round and clouting him.

"They don't look very old," Charlotte whispered.

"Well, girls used to be married off at thirteen in those days."

Charlotte wondered which days exactly. The costumes of the crowd seemed to be an anachronistic miscellany — half the cast were dressed like Chaucer's pilgrims, and the other half like the characters from a science fiction film. The director, an oldish man wearing a very obvious wig, was deep in conversation with one of the technicians. 'The Gaffer', Charlotte decided. Eventually the young man shrugged his shoulders and began propping blazing torches into metal brackets on one wall. Just beyond Romeo and Juliet, an obese man in a purple velvet cloak was practising dance steps with his partner.

"Who's that?" Charlotte asked the clown.

"Capulet," he replied, playing a tinny arpeggio and wincing. "You probably recognise him, he's been in lots of films. I'd better be off. They're doing my bit," and he strode over to an upturned half barrel, on which he sat cross-legged. He was joined by two more musicians. The dancers were forming into lines. Women in jeans were darting around picking up plastic cups and cigarette ends from the grass, and replacing pieces of fruit which had rolled on to the table. Someone was spraying the ham with varnish. When it was moved, Charlotte could see it was made of papier mâché.

Juliet was having her nose repowdered. A man in an overall was whisking through the crowd dragging a length of cable, which kept getting caught up around people's ankles. Charlotte watched, intrigued by the artifice of it all. The crew retreated to their equipment. There was a moment of stillness and silence, then a call of "Action."

The musicians struck up a reedy accompaniment as the rows of dancers, with Romeo and Juliet at opposite ends, began a stately pavan. As the two children passed each other they exchanged a look of pure yearning before being carried off by the dance.

"Cut."

The whole sequence had lasted no more than twenty seconds.

"You won't see much more than that for the next half hour," said the clown, who had made his way back to the lodge. "I should take the opportunity to get through now, if I were you."

Reluctantly she picked her way through the crowd to the stairs, stepping over coils of black flex, extension leads and boxes of lights.

Her bedroom was on the top floor and faced the road rather than the quad, so she was unable to observe any more of the theatricals. Peeling off her clothes, she stepped out of them where she stood, leaving her trousers squatting on the floor, the empty legs wrinkled into concertinas. Her eyelids were dropping with tiredness as she cleaned her teeth, spraying white droplets on to the mirror and wiping away a foaming moustache on her flannel.

Her scout had remade the bed and the sheets were smooth and starched, and smelled of soap. Before climbing in, she checked under the bed. There was nothing there but two shoes which were not partners, and a magazine. Ever since she had read *Cranford* she had been unable to get into bed without imagining a chilly hand shooting out from underneath it and seizing her ankle. She picked up the magazine, but before she had even turned the first page, her head started nodding, and she allowed herself to drift off.

She was having an erotic dream. The young Romeo was chasing her naked through the corridors of a vast castle, except that it wasn't Kevin, it was really Tyrone. Part of her knew that it was only a game, and yet part of her was scared. She was running in an agonising slow motion down endless red velvet corridors. There was a small room at the end. She scrabbled at the door and just managed to close it behind her when the Tyrone / Kevin figure arrived breathless and wild-eyed and began hammering on the wooden panels.

Charlotte sat up to find that her face was wet with tears. The hammering noise continued. She realised someone was banging on the door.

"Charlotte. Let me in. Please," a male voice was begging. She jumped out of bed, looking for something to cover herself with. She took her overcoat from the back of a chair and put it on before opening the door.

Tyrone stood there, shivering, his face greyish-white in the moonlight. His clothes were still damp and his hair had dried, unbrushed, into clumps.

Once the realisation of what he had done had actually registered in Tyrone's fuzzy consciousness, he had immediately looked around in terror, expecting to be surrounded by a lynch mob of accusing bystanders. But there was no one. Not a sound, not a movement. He looked up at the side of the college building, imagining that the noise would have brought the occupants to the windows, but the windows remained as blank and eyeless as the black sockets of a skull. Still dazed, Tyrone had hurried along to his basement room, locked himself in and put a chair against the door, before sinking back on to his bed and gazing into the shadows, wide-eyed with disbelief. He lay there, the incident running and re-running through his head until he convinced himself that it had been one of his nightmares. In order to check that it was all a dream, he ventured into the corridor. The window beside the laundry was permanently steamed up from the showers next door. Tyrone

137

rubbed a little patch with one finger and peered nervously through. He was there all right. Still in the same position, eyes open, arms thrown out as if preparing for an embrace. Tyrone leapt away from the window as if it had just burned him, and raced back to his room.

'It was an accident,' he told himself. 'An accident. Oh God . . .' He sat still in the darkness, not daring to call the police in case he was implicated, even imprisoned, and the knowledge of his own cowardice made him despise himself even more. Something made him think of Charlotte. In his desperation he began to picture her as a symbol of everything good and pure, and made his way to her room, trusting implicitly in her ability to save him.

Charlotte was confused. She could not remember which events of the previous day had actually happened and which she had dreamt. "What's going on?"

"Help me." Tyrone flung himself at her, throwing his arms around her neck and burying his face in the shaggy collar of her coat. "Please let me stay. I can't sleep."

"It's all right. It's all right." She held on to him, stroking his hair and trying to stop him from shaking. "What's the matter?"

She tried to make him look at her, but he kept his head tucked in against her neck, murmuring, "Nothing, nothing."

"Your clothes are all damp," she said, grasping the sleeve of his shirt. "No wonder you're shaking. Take them off and get into my bed to get warm." She did not press him with any more questions. She knew he still had bad nights occasionally over Sean, and assumed this was one of them. Pushing him away gently, she turned her back to allow him to strip. Pulling a couple of blankets from her wardrobe, she began to make up a bed for herself on the rug. Tyrone was in bed, the covers pulled up to his ears, watching her pad around the room barefoot, spreading cushions out on the floor and folding blankets into a sausage shape. She hung his clothes over the radiator, and still wearing her overcoat, and feeling rather foolish, wriggled between the blankets on the floor.

138

"I'm cold," Tyrone whispered desperately.

"So am I. You'll soon get warm."

He stuck one arm out of bed, holding his hand out towards her. She took it and gave it a squeeze. It was icy. He clasped his fingers around hers, refusing to let go.

"Charlie." His voice came through the darkness like a sigh, as he stroked her imprisoned hand with his thumb. "Please."

She didn't move. "What?" she asked evenly. But she knew what.

"Don't lie there miles away from me, please . . ." and as he pulled back the sheets with his free hand, she stood up, unbuttoned her overcoat, and let it fall to the floor.

16

THE first thing Alison saw when she emerged briefly from her feverish sleep was the pink and earnest face of the college chaplain. She gave a silent scream and tried to sit up, but found the sheets tucked so tightly around her that she was pinioned to the bed.

'I'm being given the last rites,' she thought wildly, as he laid the back of his hand on her forehead. It was imperative to let him know she was all right or she would be buried alive, or worse — if they found her donor card — dissected, and pieces of her redistributed all over the country. But she couldn't move, speak or even blink, paralysed in a state of semi-consciousness. After a couple of seconds her brain cleared, and by sheer force of willpower she was able to galvanise some muscles into action, jerk her head up and sink her teeth into the chaplain's large pink hand. She heard him withdraw it with a yelp, and then saw Charlotte peering anxiously over his shoulder.

Alison leant up on the pillow. "Sorry," she burbled deliriously, "I was just making sure you didn't bury me alive. I've got to get up in a minute because one of my library books is overdue." Then her face crumpled up and she said, "I want my mother, but she's in Hong Kong," before flopping backwards again into a deep sleep.

*

Charlotte had had almost as great a shock when she awoke that morning to find Tyrone's tousled head about six inches from her own.

'Oh my God.' The recollection hit her like a bucket of icy water. She lay frozen for a moment, terrified that he might wake and they would be forced to exchange some word of acknowledgement, some casual morning-after chit-chat. What could have possessed her to go to bed with him? Pity? Curiosity? Vanity? And after a funeral too. It was macabre. 'Fancy choosing a friend, of all people,' she wailed to herself. At least with a relative stranger the inevitable anti-climax could not damage any existing relationship. She desperately wanted there to be no sequel to this nocturnal visitation; an incident without consequences. 'Perhaps if I creep away before he wakes up, he will take the hint and things can carry on as if this never happened.' She eased herself carefully out of bed, disengaging her right leg from between his, picked up her overcoat from where it had been discarded the night before and, scooping up yesterday's clothes, slipped out of the door and made a dash for the bathroom.

As she soaked in a hot deep bath, she alarmed herself by imagining all sorts of disastrous scenarios. Tyrone would use the excuse of traumatic nightmares and depression as emotional blackmail every time he felt like an occasional screw. Worse still, he would feel so embarrassed and regretful about his behaviour that he would completely ignore her next time they met. She hoped he would at least have the foresight to make a quick exit from her room. She did not particularly want Patrick or Alison calling round, to be met at the door by Tyrone wearing nothing but a hand-towel and a sheepish smile.

When she returned to her room, warm and clean, she was relieved to find he had taken the opportunity of her absence to make himself scarce. He had removed all his clothes from the radiator. He had even made the bed. That was a sign of something, but whether an attempt to smooth over the incident as though it had never happened or an assertion of his newly acquired territorial rights over her bed, she couldn't be sure. Then she noticed that her washbasin had been cleaned, and the bin emptied, and realised that her scout had probably done it after all.

It was then that she heard what sounded like groaning, and the creaking of bed-springs coming through the wall from Alison's room. She held her breath. It came again, along with a faint weeping noise. Puzzled and worried, Charlotte went outside and tapped on the door.

"Alison?" Silence, then the crying started again. She decided to get a key from the lodge and break in. Whoever was in there sounded as though they needed help.

While she was in the lodge explaining the situation to the intractable porter behind the desk, the chaplain walked in.

"We don't give out spare keys to anyone except the occupant. College rules." The porter stroked his large pendulous nose.

"But this is an exception," Charlotte pleaded, daring him to say it was more than his job was worth.

"Well, I can't just let people barge into other people's bedrooms without permission. It's an invasion of privacy."

She was spared from losing her temper by the intervention of the chaplain. She explained her alarm at the strange noises coming from Alison's room, and he agreed that to use the key was to take a justifiable liberty.

"Don't worry," he reassured the indignant porter, "I take full responsibility."

Charlotte had had to restrain a snort of laughter as Alison had unexpectedly lurched forward and bitten the chaplain's avuncular hand.

"She's delirious," he announced, blushing furiously and hiding his wounded hand behind his back. "I'll fetch the nurse."

The nurse, a calm, slow-moving woman with wispy grey hair and shoes like cornish pasties, took Alison's temperature and remade the bed, the sheets having become tangled up by Alison's sudden feverish thrashings.

"Can you stay with her?" she asked Charlotte, who nodded. "Sponge her down with lukewarm water every so often, but don't let her get cold. Make sure she gets plenty of liquids," and she snapped her little bag shut and left them together. Charlotte filled the sink with warm water and looked around for a sponge. Alison did not seem to have one. Charlotte supposed an exfoliating mitt would do, as long as she didn't rub too hard. She began to wipe Alison's pale skinny arms, the water trickling off and wetting the bedclothes. She was not sure how keen she was on the role of carer — it smacked too much of angelic Victorian mothers, but this was the second time in twenty-four hours that she had found herself in the role. At least Alison was not likely to drag her into bed. The patient in question kept stirring, looking up and murmuring then relapsing into a drowsy silence. Once she seemed settled, Charlotte slipped out to make a phone call and returned to find Alison sitting up and looking with disgust at her hands which were clamped on to the top of the blankets.

"Ugh," she was saying, visibly frightened. "My hands have gone all small. My fingers are like needles," and she wagged them, and grimaced. Charlotte took hold of one.

"No they're not. You're imagining it. You're feverish."

"Oh Charlotte," she whimpered, clutching at her friend's sleeve. "Don't go," and she lay back, exhausted by the effort.

Charlotte sat beside her in the armchair all day, reading her revision notes, periodically washing down Alison's thin limbs and remaking the bed. At eight o'clock Alison sat up and asked for a cup of tea, saying she felt a little better, but by the time the kettle had boiled she had fallen asleep again, her mouth open, one arm hanging out of the bed. Charlotte tucked her back in, drank the tea herself, and made up a bed on the floor, not without a certain sense of déjà vu. She knew there was no great necessity for her to stay overnight, but she wanted to be there in case Alison woke up in the darkness, disorientated and anxious. Charlotte, on the rare occasions when she woke in the middle of the night, always had the curious feeling that she was the only person left alive. There was something unbearably lonely about sitting up waiting for the sun to rise.

The following day there was little improvement. Alison would struggle out of bed to go to the toilet opposite, but walked unsteadily, and racked the whole bed with her shivering when she returned. Intermittently, she would become quite lucid and ask for a drink or an extra blanket. It was during one of these periods that Charlotte first heard about Patrick's conversion. To begin with, she had mistaken it for more of Alison's hallucinatory ramblings, but the note on the floor had confirmed the story. Charlotte had long been sceptical about Patrick's tenacity when it came to causes and alternative lifestyles. As she had recently observed to Tyrone, Patrick's previous tastes for anarchy, astrology and self-hypnosis had passed through him with the speed of a dubious curry.

Alison gave a moan. She still had a preoccupation with the size of her hands. Sometimes she complained of their being huge and puffy, and left them dangling out of the bed as though they were too large to fit in, and at other times she rubbed them together with an expression of disgust on her face, saying "They've shrunk again. Tiny."

Charlotte suspected there must have been some major rift with Oliver to bring her back to this room, but refrained from mentioning the subject in case it distressed her. Instead she held Alison's hand, plaited her long, lank hair out of the way, and made her cups of tea which were usually abandoned after one or two sips. At seven in the evening, when Alison had finally fallen asleep after complaining about her head being too heavy for her body, Charlotte heard footsteps coming along the corridor. They passed Alison's room and stopped outside her own door. She heard a gentle tap, followed by a more insistent knocking, and eventually the footsteps retreated again.

'Tyrone,' she thought, the blood rushing to her face. Creeping downstairs to the landing, she craned through the window to see if he would emerge from the bottom of the staircase. There was no one about, but when she returned she noticed, stuffed into the handle of her door, a small bunch of wild flowers held together with an elastic band.

With a beating heart she picked them up. There were lavender, cornflowers and long-stemmed white daisies. 'He must have nicked them from the park,' she thought. A note tucked into the elastic was of such thin paper that it tore as she tried to release it. Piecing the fragments together, she read, CHARLOTTE, A FRIEND INDEED WHEN I WAS IN NEED. T.

While Charlotte searched through her own cupboards for something that would serve as a vase, surreptitiously wiping away a sentimental tear, Alison woke from her uneasy sleep to see the concerned grey eyes of her mother staring into her own. Her cry of surprise and delight made Charlotte drop the flowers and sprint next door in alarm.

She saw Vanessa Laycott, in a camel suede suit, leaning across the bed and hugging her daughter, who seemed to have instantly revived and whose face now glowed with happiness. The excitement was infectious.

"I thought you were in Hong Kong," Alison was saying.

Vanessa raised her eyes to the ceiling. "I was. It was supposed to be a World Conference on Women's Health. What a farce. Half the delegates went down with food poisoning on the first day and the key speaker from the States who I was there to interview cancelled his flight at the last minute because he was worried about terrorists. Charlotte left a message on my answering machine saying you were ill, and as soon as I heard that, I thought: 'Right, there's my excuse,' and went straight to the airport."

"You must be exhausted," said Charlotte, looking at the duty-free carrier-bag by Vanessa's feet.

Vanessa smiled. "I am. Whoever said to travel is better than to arrive obviously never went economy class." She was still holding Alison's sweaty hand. "Anyway, what's wrong with you?" she went on, smoothing a rat's tail of loose hair from her daughter's face and tucking it behind her ear.

"I don't know. Charlotte's been looking after me." Then she noticed for the first time the hastily assembled bedding on the floor. "Did you stay here last night? That was nice of you. And what day is it? I'm so confused," and she began to cry again, wiping her nose on a tiny grey shred of tissue.

"I'm here now," said Vanessa soothingly. "I'll stay until you're well again."

"But what about the exams? I've got to get up and work," Alison wailed, wriggling ineffectually against her mother's restraining grip.

"You're not getting up until your temperature is back to normal," Vanessa replied, pressing an elegantly manicured hand to Alison's burning forehead, "or you really will be ill. I'll help you work, if you like. I can read to you, and test you."

At this promise Alison calmed down, stopped twisting the sheets around in her hands, and relapsed into a resigned silence. Vanessa kissed her pale cheek, as Alison murmured, "I never thought you'd come," and wound her arms tightly around her mother's neck.

Feeling spare, Charlotte left mother and daughter together and slipped away to her own room, where she found the abandoned bunch of flowers wilting in the sunlight, the petals of the daisies already beginning to fall.

17

THE examinations were at last upon them. For the preceding fortnight, the rain had poured down relentlessly as if the sky were in mourning. For most students it was a mixed blessing — dampening the clothes and the spirits, but forcing them indoors to their books. The gutters were permanently awash, muddy water lapping over on to the pavements. A drain in the High Street was blocked, causing a large black puddle to engulf the zebra crossing. The footpaths around the meadows were sticky with mud. The river itself had flooded in places — the green field beyond Magdalen Bridge was submerged beneath a murky lake. The rising water level had inundated the rat holes and burrows along the banks, polluting the river with poisonous scum. A rower who had fallen in was rumoured to have died of a paralysing fever within twenty-four hours.

Tyrone had spent the fortnight tense with fear, imagining every knock on the door to be a summons by the police, but as each day passed it became more apparent that his encounter with the tramp had gone unobserved. There had been a brief reference in the local paper to the discovery of the body of vagrant, Archie Harris, who had fallen down a flight of steps in a fit of intoxication after stealing a bottle of whisky from the Women's Refuge in Headington. But that was all. No mention of a young man seen fleeing from the spot, or teams of forensic scientists analysing DNA prints found in traces of skin on the victim's coat.

Tyrone had only seen Charlotte on a couple of occasions since their night together. She had thanked him for the flowers, but made no further reference to the incident, and with some disappointment he had followed her lead and they had resumed their former platonic relationship, with only a trace of initial awkwardness. He congratulated himself on emerging unscathed from the affair. At least that was one problem he did not have. He still felt a gnawing guilt about the tramp which would insinuate itself into his consciousness like a bad toothache and refuse to budge. Even when his studying was at its most concentrated, an image of the slumped body, dressed in his own violet trousers and overcoat, would parade before his eyes. As the exams drew nearer, he coped by going into automatic mode, forcing himself to become a kind of learning machine, bombarding his memory with new information for sixteen hours a day, reading his notes into a tape recorder and playing them back while he ate, dressed and dropped off to sleep each night. He was so mentally and physically exhausted when the time came that he performed for the entire week in a trance-like state, having neither the energy nor the inclination to worry or reflect on his performance. This drastic approach seemed to work, however, as for the first time the jumbled miscellany of ideas which he had been carting around with him for months suddenly coalesced into a whole. He unexpectedly found a pattern behind literary history which made sense. Fragmentary opinions became coherent theories.

Discuss the significance of forgery to the writers of the Romantic period, demanded one question. Without any planning or consideration an answer seemed to flow out of him on to the page. 'Chatterton the forger,' he wrote, 'became a tragic emblem of the Romantic age — symbolising the mournful truth that all poetry is forgery. Such is the power of the language to falsify and subvert that a poem, as soon as it has its being in words, becomes a sad travesty of the visionary moment which inspired it; a betrayal of the wordless imaginative experience it was trying to commemorate.'

148

Alison, from across the ranks of black and white gowned figures, watched him in amazement as he belaboured his paper with frantic speed. Although she had recovered from her illness, and from her bitterness at the ignominious death of her erstwhile protegé, nothing had prepared her for the sheer physical effort of writing six essays a day for five days. Sometimes it required all her willpower to force her straying attention from the creeping hands of the clock back to her page. The man beside her was in a wheelchair, and had to be carried in each day in his friend's arms. She found herself watching him, wondering if he had ever made it to the upper reading room of the library, or whether he had only ever read books from the lower shelves. She was continually distracted by the performance of everyone around her. One woman had about fifty disposable biros on her desk — presumably in case forty-nine gave out one after another. One man never seemed to write anything at all. Every time she looked up he was sitting back in his chair, gazing serenely out of the window. And some people covered so much paper. There always seemed to be a forest of arms raised for a second booklet before she was even half-way through her first. She tried increasing the size of her already generous scrawl but it made little difference. She had tried to take the edge off her anxiety by convincing herself that it would not matter if she failed. Then anything better would be a bonus. But at the back of her mind she knew she would be bitterly disappointed with anything less than the best. If Oliver had managed a First, so could she. She knew it was unhealthy, but both she and Charlotte were success junkies, egging each other on to ever higher goals in a punishing crusade against under-achievement. Two desks away she could see Charlotte's bowed head, her right arm working away.

Once the exams actually arrived Charlotte felt she could relax and even enjoy them in a masochistic way. She was doubly relieved that, thanks to her smooth handling of the whole business with Tyrone, there had been no emotional repercussions to interfere with her study. It was just as she had always suspected. As long as both parties were sensible, it was possible to have a one-off fling with a good friend without things getting messy and problematic. Now that was settled, she felt safe to dismiss all non-academic considerations from her mind. She found herself looking forward to each day's paper like an actor who, after months of rehearsal, longs for the applause of the opening night. Although she could not imagine any of the dons, who tiptoed up and down the rows of chairs each day distributing paper, giving any of her essays a standing ovation, it was sufficient to know that they would be read. Writing itself was also a great release. Like lancing a wound, it was a relief to spill out the ideas that she had been imprisoning in her head for the last three years. She was surprised how easily it all came to her. It was as though something had been germinating within her. New ideas seemed to divide and multiply as she wrote, faster than she could even think, as if her hand was being fed directly by her subconscious without the intervention of deliberate thought. It was exhilarating, but agonising too — the fear that this unknown source of inspiration would suddenly desert her, leaving her becalmed on a dark and empty sea. But it never did. Once, during her Wordsworth paper, a dog had started barking in the courtyard below, yapping away to an insistent rhythm until all the candidates had been forced to acknowledge it, smirking, laughing and fidgeting in their seats. Eventually, when things had quietened down again, one of the examiners could be heard outside saying "Would you mind keeping your dog quiet," and that had set people off again, but not even this had put Charlotte off her stride. Then almost before it had started, it was time for the last paper, and inside the hall there was a palpable tremor of excitement and anticipation. The apparently interminable rain had stopped at lunchtime and a watery blue sky was emerging as the candidates filed in for their final exam. Time seemed to have a scale of its own inside the vast, silent room. The first two hours plodded by with painful slowness, then the minutes seemed to career past. Charlotte's euphoria, as the clock registered five minutes to go, was almost unbearable. She wanted to halt there, poised on the brink of freedom, to savour the feeling of completion, survival, of indescribable lightness. Then it was all over and the chief examiner was congratulating them, and they were swept out on to the street in a body. There were crowds of people waiting around the building, choking up the pavement, being herded along by weary proctors. She was being patted on the back, her hair ruffled by friends and fellow students, then Tyrone and Alison were beside her and they were hugging each other and laughing in the bright sunlight.

18

❧❦❧

"WHEN can we fly the balloon?" Patrick asked.

"Tomorrow, if it's not raining," Greg answered. Patrick looked out at the boiling clouds which were forming with punishing regularity above the steaming trees on the hills.

"It won't rain," he said firmly.

They had left Oxford the day after Patrick had arrived on the doorstep of the Brotherhood's commune, and had been living in the tiny cottage in Powys ever since. The cottage was an old stone farmhouse in a valley, half a mile down a rutted muddy track. It had nothing that might be termed a facility — no electricity, plumbing or running water.

"What if I'm suddenly taken ill?" Patrick had asked, looking uneasily around for the phone.

"I'll heal you," came the reply.

Patrick could see why new recruits were brought there — the change in lifestyle was so dramatic that even his most basic expectations were undermined, and the simplest habits had to be relearned. There was no time to lament the lack of ready-made entertainment; the business of merely living took up all their time. For example, it took over an hour to have a bath. The water had to be collected from a trough into which the stream had been diverted on its way down the valley, and heated in a copper pot on the range. The process was repeated until the enamel bath in the second of the two ground-floor rooms was half full. There was a plastic chemical toilet in the shed tacked on to the side of the house, and a fresh pit had to be dug every few days into which it could be emptied. Every second day they would walk the half-mile down the valley to the grocer's in the village, to refill a two-gallon water bottle for cooking and drinking. They would wheel it back in an old wooden barrow, along with any food they had bought. In spite of the fine weather, the stone walls and floors made the place permanently cold, and the range had to be kept alight more or less constantly. Its insatiable appetite for fuel meant that at least an hour each day was spent chopping logs and taking the barrow up into the woods to collect fallen branches. The floors had to be swept daily as the clayey mud from the lane, which they inevitably brought in on their shoes, dried to a thin film of ochre dust. Greg also liked to make fresh bread every morning, folding and kneading the dough at the large table beside the bath and baking it in the tiny oven in the range. As they had brought few clothes with them, there was a continual supply of washing to be done. Patrick rigged up a line between two trees with some whiskery string he had found in the woodshed. As soon as the dry clothes were taken down, stiff and cool and smelling of fresh air, there always seemed to be a new lot of wet ones to take their place.

They shared the jobs equally, alternating their tasks each day or two. At first Patrick had been embarrassed at the thought of Greg washing his underpants for him, but events soon forced him to overcome his squeamishness. One night, after eating some dubious mushrooms from the woods, he found himself with a pitiless and very audible attack of diarrhoea. On his third descent, when he actually made it as far as the freezing black hell-hole beneath the bedroom window, Greg followed him, and stood in the doorway holding a candle so that Patrick could find the toilet seat without further casualty. After groaning over a chemi-loo in a damp little shed at three in the morning, in full view of

Greg, he did not feel he really had any more inhibitions to lose. Greg, to his credit, had played his part with the impassive indifference of a nurse. He had even cleaned up the near misses before Patrick awoke the next day.

Then there was the demanding vegetable garden behind the house which required regular weeding. Only a chicken-wire fence separated the cultivated area from the wilderness beyond. This proved no barrier to the dandelions, nettles and bindweed which persistently strayed among the seedlings, strangling them. There were rows of cabbages, cauliflowers and onions, lettuces and greens to be harvested.

"Brother Thomas planted them in the spring, when he was here on retreat," Greg explained. Whoever stayed at the cottage was expected to eat the ripe vegetables and plant a new batch in their place. Patrick enjoyed doing the garden, loosening the clods of earth, pulling out the weeds and turning the soil over. It occurred to him, as he made an indentation in the ground with a rake and dropped carrot seed into it, that he had never before eaten a home-grown vegetable. There was something profoundly satisfying about being so close to the ground. Instead of standing up and prodding the soil with a long-handled hoe, Patrick preferred to squat down and work with his hands, feeling the warm damp earth between his fingers and under his nails. Growing vegetables, he decided, was like a diluted form of childcare. When he said this to Greg, as they were tying a cat's cradle of fine wool between stakes to protect the new seeds, Greg became interested. "I always feel it's just another example of our exclusion. We merely deposit the seed and hover anxiously on the border, cut off from the real business of reproduction. I often think that is why men have always tried to appropriate the arts for themselves. A sort of desperate stab at creativity, to compensate for the fact that in the most important creative act we are just casual participants."

Patrick wondered about this. Were Shakespeare's plays, Beethoven's symphonies, Leonardo da Vinci's paintings all expressions of thwarted womb envy? It would go some way to explain the lamentable fate of mothers in Shakespeare,

154

he supposed. Even those who made it into the dramatis personae seemed to end up poisoned, butchered or stuck on a plinth. He was wondering whether there was a thesis topic in there somewhere, but Greg had moved on.

"Vegetables are very embryonic-looking, aren't they?" he was saying, squatting over a cabbage and stroking its dome-shaped head. "Isn't this like a baby's skull, laced with veins, and this could be a brain?" He spread open the leaves surrounding a white cauliflower.

Patrick was pulling up a handful of carrots by their green fronds. Some were not fully grown, but were pale, ribbed and slender, like tiny fingers. Greg took one from him, and brushed the dirt off before examining it. "This one even has a knuckle," he observed, and replanted it at the end of the row.

Patrick had taken some time to adapt to this new routine. It was difficult to discard the sense of haste and urgency which had accompanied every move in his previous life. One morning during the first week, Greg had come into the kitchen to find him washing out the sheets in cold water, his hands almost purple with cold.

"Why aren't you using hot water?" he had asked.

"It takes too long to heat up on the stove," Patrick had replied.

"Too long for what?"

Now he had been there for over a month, Patrick was beginning to understand the logic of Greg's insistence that the daily tasks were to be done at a steady, comfortable pace and strictly one at a time. He had stopped feeling guilty every time he was forced to sit waiting for the copper pot to boil, but used the time to meditate instead. Greg was emphatic that it was cutting corners and hurrying that turned a satisfying task into a chore. As soon as Patrick had grasped that these daily jobs were to be the fabric of his life rather than the messy oil on the machinery, he was able to perform them with renewed concentration and pleasure.

In the evenings when the meal was over and cleared away, and the gas lamp lit and whining, they would sit in front of the range together. There was one tall wooden bench like a church pew, a low table made of a horizontal slice through an oak tree, and a sagging armchair whose green stippled cover was balding around the arms. Patrick could imagine a series of anxious novices picking away nervously at the material while they listened to the resident brother's exposition of the necessities of communal life. Greg would read, usually a work of Eastern mysticism. Some nights he would take the large pine hand loom from the kitchen cupboard, and work away at a natural wool rug that was gradually emerging. It had been started the previous visit by Brother Marcus who had once run a craft shop in Grasmere. It was hoped that it would eventually be long enough to form a rough carpet for the narrow wooden staircase to the upper floor.

Patrick spent much of this time gazing into the fire which was raging away behind the sooty glass door of the range, and thinking. He had felt a new sense of balance and weightlessness since his arrival. Perhaps it was the change of diet, he thought. Or his withdrawal from stressful situations. Whatever it was, his mind no longer felt cluttered with half-formed worries. It was as if he had swept up and disposed of all the mental debris which had been hampering him. He had tried to keep a journal during the first fortnight, but the weeks followed such a similar pattern that he found himself writing 'see Monday', 'see Tuesday', as an indicator of the day's activities. He had tried changing it to a diary of his thoughts and feelings, but his style immediately became tortured and self-conscious and horribly embellished – playing up to an imaginary reader until he realised that the person he was writing about was not himself at all, but a totally fictional character. Eventually he had decided that the diary was a perfidious form anyway – posturing as a private record but all the time demanding, implying, the presence of a reader – so he had thrown it on the fire. Besides, self-expression smacked too much of individualism and egotism, and he sensed Greg's approval as they watched the blue exercise book curl up and shrivel into black tissue. Most of the material sacrifices associated with the way of the Brotherhood did not cause Patrick a moment's regret — which, he supposed, meant that they were not proper sacrifices. It had been no hardship to surrender exclusive rights to his few possessions — except his toothbrush, over which he assumed he could still retain sovereignty. He had let Greg cut his hair to a prickly half an inch all over, and after one quick glance at his reflection in the water trough, tried to dismiss his appearance from his thoughts. He did not even mind Greg playing his flute, which he did surprisingly well. Greg also had a set of pan pipes which he would sometimes play while he went off into the forest looking for firewood. The mournful call could be heard from several fields away and Patrick occasionally caught a faint echo of the music while he worked in the garden. The sound haunted him. There was something pagan and sensuous about it which seemed to sit uneasily alongside Greg's glacial asceticism.

His only reservation about the whole Brotherhood system concerned the idea of suspending the personality. Greg's chilly neutrality baffled him. Greg was easy enough to live with. He had no irritating habits, but he was, at the same time, annoyingly inaccessible, as though the real man was submerged beneath layers and layers of self-discipline. His reactions, it seemed to Patrick, were never spontaneous but always dictated by an acquired sense of how a Brother ought to respond. Talking to Greg was rather like interviewing a politician: his answers were cautious, predictable and impersonal, revealing nothing more than the party line. Patrick wondered whether chipping away at the strata would eventually unearth a core of boiling individuality, or whether there would just be layers all the way through. Patrick did not want to be leached of every drop of his personality. He valued his sense of self, the awareness of the something that made him Patrick rather than anyone else, and sensed that the loss of this perception involved straying across the blurred dividing line between sanity and madness. He tried to explain this to Greg one afternoon when they were pushing

157

the barrow back from the village. The grocer had given them piles of old newspapers for the fire, as well as their regular canister of drinking water, and it took one of them at each handle to manoeuvre the cart back along the track. It was a squally day and the clouds were low and threatening. Recent rain had filled the ruts in the road with what looked like weak tea, and the clay was treacherously slippery one moment and impossibly sticky the next.

"We don't require you to renounce your sanity," Greg was saying, hopping on one foot and retrieving his other shoe from the mud with a squelch. "Of course you must be confident of your identity. What you want to avoid," he went on, launching himself once more at the resisting barrow, "is the destructive habit of stamping everything you say and do with your own personality. If a stranger were to come to the Brotherhood for a day, the most serene, enlightened and truly fulfilled of us would be the one the stranger never even noticed. That is the sort of invisibility we must all aim for."

"But if I hadn't noticed you — if you hadn't forced your way into my consciousness, I wouldn't be here now, would I?"

They were distracted from this conversation by the barrow slipping off one of the ridges into a rut and refusing to budge. It was only later, after they had built up a ramp of stone slabs under the wheels, gently eased the barrow back on to the solid crests of the track and coaxed it carefully home, that Patrick realised he had not received an answer.

It was on one of these many walks that Patrick had first had the idea of making an air balloon. Before breakfast one morning the two men had walked down into the village to buy some more flour and yeast for baking. The sun had just risen, and the sky was a pale washed-out blue. The hem of Greg's gown and the frayed ends of Patrick's jeans were soaked with dew as they swished through the tall grass alongside the track. A cow stood at the edge of the field staring at them insolently over the barbed-wire fence. Patrick approached it with a handful of grass, but it rolled its eyes in alarm, jerked its head up and lurched off across the paddock to the rest of the herd.

The village consisted of a nucleus of cottages beside a pond, a church, a pub, a telephone box and a few shops. Patrick was amazed that any of them made enough money to survive. There was never a customer in sight. There was the grocery store, which they patronised quite frequently and in which they were warmly welcomed, the owner, a local representative of the RSPCA, being under the mistaken impression that they belonged to an order of Franciscans. Beyond the grocer's was a post office, which also sold a curious variety of items apparently exclusive to rural post offices, and which fell into no discernible category. There was a cardboard sheet of multi-coloured bouncing balls behind cellophane bubbles, like a giant packet of contraceptives, and gold and silver cake candle-holders which could be bought individually or in packets of twenty-four. In the centre of the shop was a stand of diaries and calendars reduced to half price in recognition of the fact that half the year had elapsed. Balanced on the top were turquoise boxes of confetti, and cartons of wax crayons, the smell of which instantly transported Patrick back to his junior school, whose corridors had always hung with the combined odours of crayon, disinfectant, and pools of sick reeking beneath their discreet covering of sawdust.

Next to the post office was a chemist which never seemed to be open, a butcher's, a bakery, a couple of cafés and, standing on its own at the corner of a terrace, the village junkshop. A sign above the grubby window optimistically stated ICARUS ANTIQUES and in smaller letters, as if an afterthought, AND SHOE REPAIRS. In the window was a miscellany of faded and tatty white elephants: grubby crocheted tablemats, splitting basketweave plant-holders, Jubilee ashtrays, an unsteady nest of chipboard tables, several tarnished silver coffee pots, a rack of gilt picture frames, and a large ornamental amphora with a pair of grotesque gold handles, like great crinkly ears, jutting out either side.

Outside on a bench was a row of secondhand books, only a handful of which Patrick recognised. On this particular morning, he was not sure why — it could have been the sunshine, or the smell of hot bread issuing from the bakery — he felt particularly creative. He found himself scouring the shop windows for something his imagination could latch on to. Since he had aborted his journal, he had done nothing but practical chores apart from playing a few bars on the flute, or taking an occasional turn at the hand loom.

"I feel like doing something different today, maybe some painting or something," he said to Greg, who was busy trying to stop the flour leaking out of a split in the bag.

"You could try painting the outside of the house," came the reply. "There's some paint and brushes in the woodshed."

Patrick was not listening. Behind the window of Icarus Antiques was suspended a new acquisition. Dangling from a hook above the rickety tables was a hand-made miniature air balloon about one foot across, attached to a square cane basket by an intricate arrangement of rigging. There was even a tiny figure leaning out, one arm raised in salute. The image of a hot-air balloon amongst this shabby collection of refuse masquerading as antiques was so romantic, so unexpected, that Patrick was immediately fired with enthusiasm to build one of his own. Not, he reassured Greg, a full-sized one. It would only have to be large enough to lift its own fuel supply. Rootless wandering by proxy was enough for him.

What came to be known locally as the 'balloon incident' began that same evening, when Patrick brought some scissors and gardening wire in from the woodshed and constructed a light frame, about four feet in diameter. Although he knew Greg would not refuse him money for materials, he was relieved to find, beneath the film of cobwebs in the shed, dusty and neglected versions of everything he was likely to need. His intention was to make the balloon itself as spherical as possible. An inverted paper sack would have floated as readily but he wanted it to resemble the real thing.

During the following week Patrick worked on his project each night after dinner, while Greg accompanied him on the pan pipes or rolled the shuttle back and forth across the loom. "I wonder if I will finish this stair carpet before you finish your balloon," Greg mused, watching Patrick dipping a sheet of newspaper into a bucket of flour and water paste and plastering it across the wire frame.

Patrick picked up another sheet. A topless girl pouted at him across the handlebars of a motorbike. He discarded it hastily and selected a more innocent-looking crossword before smearing it with glue. "I don't think this unrefined flour is really the thing for papier mâché," he observed. It had hardened in places to a rough gritty finish.

By the following morning, the membrane of glutinous pulp had dried to a crisp, slightly wizened shell. Patrick found three pots of enamel paint in the shed — the previous occupant had clearly been a model aeroplane enthusiast. With a stiff, bristly brush he daubed the newsprint with blue and green splodges. He was saving the gold for the basket, which was made from an old paint pot, washed and punctured around the rim.

One evening towards the end of their stay, Patrick called Greg in from the kitchen, where the latter had been hanging bunches of mint, lemon balm and thyme to dry in the window. He was proudly holding the finished balloon, from which a gold basket was suspended, the words 10% EXTRA FREE clearly visible through the paint.

"It looks like the globe," said Greg, walking around it admiringly. "These wrinkles could even represent the relief except some of them are in the sea."

"When shall we fly it?" Patrick asked, deferring to his sense that Greg was, after all, the leader.

"Tomorrow, if it's not raining."

"It won't rain," Patrick said firmly.

It poured down all the next day, forcing them to abandon the launch and resume their normal routine. Even Greg seemed preoccupied. Patrick was amazed at his own inability to concentrate. He kept drifting off into fantasies of flight and freedom, his imagination soaring away in advance of his creation. Prior to his arrival at the cottage, such a minute event would hardly have registered a flicker of interest. 'It just shows,' he thought, 'how one's standards change.' He was not sure whether they had been raised or lowered – perhaps they had just been moved sideways.

The morning after, Patrick and Greg were awakened by unusually loud bleating. Crawling off his mattress to the window, Patrick saw a dozen sheep systematically cropping the vegetable patch. Greg joined him at the window and burst out laughing. "They must have broken through one of the fences. We'd better round them up. This'll be fun."

After half an hour of chasing, cajoling and, on Patrick's part, swearing, all but one of the sheep had been herded back into their field. They approached the final escapee.

"This way," said Greg with quiet authority, pointing at the hole in the fence.

"Come here, you stupid bugger," Patrick howled, as the shaggy animal blundered between them. It took a further twenty minutes before they had the terrified creature cornered and were able to coax it along towards the opening, waving their arms menacingly whenever it threatened to bolt.

"At least it's fine weather for the maiden voyage," Greg remarked, as they made temporary repairs to the farmer's fence to prevent any further assaults on the garden. Patrick looked around. The ground was still wet but the sky was blue, except in the distance over the hills where white bubbly clouds hovered like another herd of itinerant sheep. There was a southerly wind blowing, which meant that the balloon would be carried across the valley to the hills rather than down towards the village. The breeze was brisk without being gusty. Conditions were perfect.

His eagerness to put his handiwork to the test was soon dampened when, on inspection, the tin of methylated spirit on which he had been relying for fuel proved to have only two inches of liquid in the bottom.

"It's never going to be able to circumnavigate the globe on that," Patrick said, visibly disappointed, swilling the purple fluid around in the can.

Greg untied the washing line, knotted one end to the

basket which was lying between them on the grass, and wound the free end around his wrist.

"Let's just see if it even gets airborne," he suggested. Patrick poured the dribble of methylated spirit into the gold tin, lit it quickly and held the neck of the balloon directly above the flame. Slowly, incredibly, it began to nudge against his hands and to rise gently and then more urgently, until the string tightened with a snap and the balloon was bobbing and swaying on the end of the leash directly above their heads.

"It works," said Greg in disbelief, tugging at the washing line and feeling the resistance as the swollen paper shell wobbled and tugged back.

"Don't let go," ordered Patrick, disappearing in the direction of the shed and returning with an old jar of turpentine. "This might work."

Greg reeled in the balloon doubtfully. There was a picture of a flame on the bottle with a large orange and black cross and a skull beside it. It looked fairly unequivocal. "I don't think . . ." was all he managed to say before Patrick emptied the entire jar into the already burning can. It ignited with a boom, and Greg, injudiciously downwind, found himself inhaling a dense cloud of acrid black smoke. Gasping and leaping aside, he let go of the washing line, just as the wind with predictable perversity, changed direction, sending the smoking globe careering towards the village.

Through watering eyes, the two men looked at each other and then at the blue and green orb with its attendant train of poisonous stinking fog, as it floated high above them on direct course for the distant cluster of shops and houses. Then without a word, they simultaneously broke into a run and raced down the track after it, splashing and slithering on the clay.

"Please, please," Patrick prayed, as if only a colossal act of willpower would keep the balloon airborne. "Please don't fall." He had wanted so much for it to soar effortlessly up into the clouds but already it was clear that it was losing height.

A small crowd of villagers were standing on the green outside the church when the apparition first drifted into view. As Greg and Patrick reached the main street, they could see shopkeepers emerging from their doorways and following the pointing fingers of the crowd with their eyes. The two men stood helplessly in the middle of the road at a discreet distance from the spectators, watching as the balloon skimmed over the church roof leaving a veil of smoke hanging in its wake.

"What on earth is it?" they could hear one elderly woman asking, squinting upwards and shielding her face from the sun.

"It'll never clear the shops," another observed.

"Go on, go on," Patrick begged silently, urging it to prove them wrong and rise above the rooftops and sail away into the infinite expanse beyond.

"Oh-oh," he heard Greg say, as it scraped the chimney pot of the chemist's shop, before dragging the resisting gold paint pot along the guttering of Icarus Antiques and Shoe Repairs, where it became wedged. The dented blue and green globe tugged ineffectually against this unexpected anchoring, and wavered elegantly for a moment before sagging fatally across the mouth of the fuel container and bursting into flames. As the volunteer fire service came clanging down the main street, scattering the onlookers, Patrick saw that Greg was shaking with silent hysterics, and then he too saw the funny side and joined in, until their laughter rang out above the dying wail of the siren. But in spite of this, as he watched his balloon straining to dislodge its basket from the guttering and finally expiring in a ball of fire, he had felt an almost premonitory sense of despair.

19

    ❧❧❧

"Y OU'RE pregnant."

    'Oh dear,' thought Charlotte, looking at the green leather of the desk and then at the doctor's red and black tie. 'How banal.' But instead she said, "Are you sure?"

She had only gone to see him because of a sore throat, but he was young and sympathetic, and had talked her into manifesting exhaustion, loss of appetite, unpredictable mood swings and a whole host of symptoms on top. Now the samples had come back and here she was sitting on a hard chair looking across his charcoal grey 100% pure wool sleeve at a smiling photograph of his wife in an oval frame.

"But I've been on the pill for three years."

The doctor gave her a rueful smile. "I'm sorry. The pill is only 99·9 per cent effective. I'm sure you realise that the only foolproof form of contraception is abstinence." For a second he sounded like her granny. "But if it's what you want, I'll be more than happy to arrange a termination for you."

'More than happy?' Charlotte thought, as she made her way slowly through the market afterwards. The day before she had felt just fine. Today she knew she was pregnant, and that awareness made all the difference. Although it could only be six weeks, she felt she must already be visibly swollen and ticking like a time bomb. She also found it hard to register any of the appropriate reactions — horror, panic, remorse. All she could manage was incredulity and an objective sense of interest.

'I have become a cliché,' was her main thought. She felt dangerously detached. On her aimless perambulation through the market, she became more and more preoccupied with the statistical audacity of her situation. 99·9 per cent safe, the doctor had said. But that was clearly misleading. For 99·9 per cent of women it was 100 per cent safe, and for the poor old buggers in the ·1 per cent of the pie chart it was 100 per cent useless.

'So,' she thought, as she climbed the stairs to Rita's coffee shop, 'I am to have an abortion.' She wondered what her eleven-year-old self, the moral diarist who considered hair-dye a crime against humanity, would have made of it. She had now broken every single decree on her list — including the final and most heinous one of 'getting herself pregnant'. She could imagine the little girl looking at her down the corridor of years, shaking her head sadly like a miniature maiden aunt. It was a strange and alienating experience to have mislaid her conscience, discarded it somewhere along with her junior bras and brace. All she could concentrate on was the mechanics of it all — the biology. Charlotte's acquaintance with the procedure of abortion was sketchy, culled mostly from inattentive readings of women's health manuals and the blood-spattered idiom of popular fiction. Over her coffee and cream gateaux ('eating for two now,' she thought blackly) she tried to imagine exactly what they would do to her — they being the teams of men and women in masks and squeaking sterile rubber gloves — but drew a blank. She tried to remember any incidents of abortion she had read about. There didn't seem to be any in Literature with a capital L. Macduff was from his mother's womb untimely ripp'd, which she supposed made him an abortion gone horribly wrong, but he was the only one she could think of. It seemed strange that there was such an omission. Only by counting stillbirths and infanticide did any sort of bibliography emerge at all. It was probably that such things were not written or even thought about before the twentieth century, she decided.

Anyway, it was certainly not the sort of thing which happened to a heroine.

Out-Patients. Incredible, she thought, as she sat in a yellow plastic chair in the waiting room reading the anti-smoking posters. It's just like going to the dentist, or having a verruca dug out. In and out without so much as a bed-bath or a dollop of institution mash. She hoped it was a result of the simplicity of the operation rather than a lack of beds. She had brought a book to read but was unable to concentrate — there was too much else to look at. An old man with a rattling cough kept barking and spitting into his handkerchief. Charlotte felt sick. There were half a dozen young women besides herself in the room. One was flicking through a magazine, staring blankly past the pages. All abortions, Charlotte decided. It's going to be like a production line in there. In and out with barely enough time to dunk the instruments in hot water before the next one arrives.

She had told no one. Alison had gone on holiday to Florence with Vanessa as soon as the exams had finished, and was therefore unavailable as a prop. Patrick, of whom nothing had been heard, was presumably still buried in the Welsh countryside. Tyrone, still at large, drifting, aimless, awaiting, she presumed, his inevitable Third, was out of the question. She could never admit to him that what had begun as a no-strings affair suddenly threatened to grow an umbilical cord; that for a while at least there existed the promise of a living synthesis of the two of them, capable of pitching them both into the next generation.

A doctor in a spotless white coat came striding through the double doors, a nurse walking deferentially one pace behind as she addressed him.

"I haven't slept for forty-eight hours," Charlotte heard him say with a shrug, as they marched at a brisk pace down the long corridor to the next set of swing doors, which creaked back and forward drowning her reply. Several of the patients around Charlotte exchanged anxious glances. She suddenly had the strangest feeling that she was outside her own body, slightly above it, looking down at herself in the warm, hushed waiting-room. She was mesmerised by the minutest details of her surroundings — the torn corner of a poster advertising measles vaccinations, a tiny brown stain on the tie of the old man next to her, the way her foot just fitted between the outline of a floor tile, the receptionist's head and shoulders framed in the hatch like a portrait, and the way her fragile gold necklace was caught up in the whiskers of her cardigan. Charlotte longed to get up and tweak it free.

Then a nurse appeared, holding a piece of paper, glancing across the rows of expectant faces. "Charlotte Rowley," she said, raising her plucked eyebrows, and Charlotte could feel in the chilly tone of her voice the scrape of cold metal.

Charlotte stood on the threshold of Out-Patients, her coat buttoned tightly to the neck. She was wearing two bulky sanitary towels which felt like a roll of loft insulation between her thighs. It reminded her of her schooldays — pink in the face and squirming before the school nurse who would send her away with a small cardboard box from which a compressed towel would balloon, on its release, like a life-raft.

Clasping her handbag as if it was the only possession she had, she walked gingerly, almost bow-legged, across the forecourt to the pavement. In spite of the blue sky there was a glacial chill in the air which made her shrink even further into herself. The sense of deliverance which she had anticipated would come with her departure from hospital eluded her as she stood at the bus stop. Instead there was an emptiness, a greyness about everything. 'I have been hollowed out,' she thought. 'Like a clay model.'

Somewhere a bell rang, and a moment later a small boy in school uniform, a tiny tie on elastic twisted half-way around his collar, came trotting along weighed down by an enormous bag. On his head was a paper crown, evidently newly made, with crayonned triangles in blue and green around the sides.

He was having difficulty keeping it on. Each time he let go to get a firmer grip on the bag, the wind caught it, and he would clutch at it and pull it back on. This pantomime continued for about a hundred yards, until a sudden gust of wind blew it back along the pavement. Putting his hands to his head too late, and dropping his bag, the little boy ran after the crown which was now bowling along in the dust with crisp packets, bus tickets and grubby flower petals. As soon as he reached it, the wind would whip it further away. As Charlotte watched, the paper crown hesitated for a moment on the kerb before being swept into the path of an oncoming car which crushed it. The boy looked at the crumpled remains in disbelief for a second, and then burst into uninhibited sobs.

For Charlotte too, at last, the tears came. For the first time since she had discovered she was pregnant, her bleak sense of uninvolvement left her, and she stood at the bus stop crying openly. It was such a relief to feel her humanity restored to her, to feel tears on her cheeks, that they seemed as miraculous and welcome as an oasis in a parched and stony desert.

20

❧❧

"PERHAPS you should have stuck to weaving?" Greg was saying, running his fingers through Patrick's hair to relieve a headache.

After enduring a humiliating lecture from the chief volunteer fire-fighter about the abuse of inflammable materials, they had trudged back to the cottage empty-handed. The balloon had been reduced to a charred wire skeleton, to which the odd shred of blackened paper still clung, fluttering feebly in the breeze.

"The local newspaper is bound to do a story about it," Greg had said, as soon as they were out of earshot of the bystanders. "They'll probably send someone round to interview you. No doubt we will be portrayed as a couple of amiable cranks."

Patrick cringed. The thought of such trivial notoriety reminded him of Boris and Blitz stain remover. He could imagine exactly how the *Llarno Gazette* would run the story.

BALLOON GOES UP ⌐ IN SMOKE!

Local Llarno residents were startled yesterday by the sight of a burning hot air balloon drifting down their main street. Mr Reg Grogan, who was fixing a slate on the Post Office roof, alerted local firefighters as the balloon became wedged in the gutter of the Icarus Antique Shop. Mr Arthur Turpin, chief volunteer fire-fighter, arrived on the scene to put out the blaze. The balloon was the property of the Brotherhood of Enlightenment, a small spiritual community who took over Bell's farmhouse three years ago. The launch of a smoking balloon is believed to be a part of their religious observances. Patrick Weston, novice both in enlightenment and aviation, warned locals that next year would be the Brotherhood's official 'Year of the Rocket'.

His headache had come on as soon as they had arrived home. It was now dark outside, and the thumping in his temples still did not seem to be responding to any of Greg's remedies. Greg's original suggestion of wearing a sprig of thyme around his neck and lying head downmost on a plank raised at one end, produced no result other than dizziness. Patrick longed for an aspirin. Greg had then decided that a scalp massage would relieve the tension.

"Pain-killers just alleviate the symptoms — they don't cure the problem," he said stroking Patrick's head with a light combing motion from forehead to neck. When he reached the nape he would throw his hands out to the side, flicking his fingers as though trying to dislodge something unpleasant from under his nails.

"Have I got dandruff or something?" Patrick asked in alarm, craning his head round.

"No. This is supposed to ease the pressure. Imagine I'm absorbing all the pain into my fingers and then dispersing it."

After ten minutes Patrick grudgingly admitted that he was feeling slightly better. "We've only got another few days here," he was thinking aloud.

"Yes." Greg sounded almost wistful. Slipping his hands inside Patrick's shirt to his shoulders, he began to massage them gently.

"This time next week we will be back in Oxford."

"Yes, yes." Again the same sad thoughtful tone. Patrick felt Greg's fingers tighten. Then, afterwards he could not quite believe it had happened, Greg, his hands still gripping

171

Patrick by the shoulders, reached down and kissed him lightly on the back of the neck. No sooner had he done it, than he straightened up and disappeared into the kitchen and could be heard clattering around with the water jug and bowl.

It had been so unexpected, so alien to Greg's normal behaviour that Patrick, as he listened to the splash of the water, wondered whether he could possibly have imagined the whole thing. He sat there, stunned, his mouth dry, gazing vacantly into the fire. He felt as though he had been kicked in the ribs. It was as astounding as being propositioned by the College Chaplain, or Dr Beamish. He could not bring himself to do anything more than nod as Greg came out of the kitchen wiping his face on his sleeve and said, quite normally, "I'm off to bed now," before mounting the creaking staircase.

'My God,' thought Patrick, pacing up and down in front of the fire. 'I must be going mad. Pull yourself together. He was probably just being brotherly.' He stood there for five minutes or so until he could no longer hear any noise from upstairs. Then, sweating profusely, he extinguished the lamp, picked up a candle and crept up the stairs, hoping to find Greg already asleep. Peering into the gloom, he could see that both mattresses were empty. Greg was standing at the window, silhouetted against the violet of the sky. The flickering candlelight cast huge looming shadows over the uneven plaster walls. Greg turned and took a step towards him, his face ashen.

"Patrick . . ." he said in a strangulated voice, grasping his friend's arm and making the flame waver. Patrick stood gaping at him across the candle, sure that his heart had stopped beating. He was paralysed, suspended in the darkness as though the air was as thick as glycerine.

"I thought, I wondered . . ." Greg was staring searchingly into his eyes now as if trying to retrieve some lost object from the bottom of a pool. "If you wanted to, we might spend the night together," and he reached out hesitantly and touched Patrick's burning cheek.

Seeing Patrick's look of dismay he released him and shrank

back again, his face taking on a tortured expression. "I'm sorry. I'm sorry. I just thought that it might help us to celebrate our spiritual relationship. But if you don't want to, then please don't feel ..." His voice became more desperate and groping.

It was not glycerine now but endless empty space, and Patrick felt himself falling through it. His hand was hurting. He looked down and realised he had poured boiling hot wax all over it. Greg turned away to the window again and threw it open, sending a draught across the room which extinguished the candle. He leaned out, breathing deeply, before facing Patrick again.

"We'd better go to sleep," he said in his controlled, authoritative voice. His face had resumed its mask-like opacity.

"But Greg," Patrick had found his voice at last. Now that they could not see each other's faces so clearly it was easier. "I don't understand." He struggled for words. In the last few minutes everything seemed to have shifted its perspective, and he could feel a terrible crisis about to be unleashed. "I thought this was a celibate order. You can't really mean all that about improving spiritual closeness. It's against your vows. I mean is it or isn't it?" he floundered.

Greg was silent for a second, then said, very quietly, "Yes, of course it is," and sat down cross-legged on the mattress, his head bowed. "Please don't feel disgusted with me. I didn't want to embarrass you. Please just forget this whole thing. I promise I will never give you any cause to remember it again. I need some time alone on retreat, I think, to cure myself."

"But Greg," Patrick protested. "Being gay isn't something you need to cure. You must leave the Brotherhood — you can't stay in a celibate order and just hope to suppress everything. You must leave. You'll find a partner ..." He was almost incoherent with frustration.

"I don't want a *partner*," the words floated through the darkness towards him like moths. "It was just you." And when he said that, it all became clear to Patrick at last. He

173

had uncovered that 'something' which inspired Greg, that something beneath all the layers which had made his asceticism easy to bear. And it had been him. Patrick.

His mouth dried up. "I'm sorry. I don't feel the same. I could only ever think of you as a Brother, and a friend. But you'll meet someone else. I'm nothing," and for once he believed in his own hollowness.

Greg shook his head. "Do you remember our first meeting at Boris's? I knew then I'd found you. I thought you felt it too."

"I did feel . . . that our meeting was significant, but not in that way. I saw you as someone who could be a mentor, and give my life some direction . . ." It was agony for Patrick to have to open himself out in this way, but it seemed an act of cruelty to remain aloof and guarded while Greg was mining the depths of his own heart.

"I'll never forget that day at Boris's," Greg went on in a low voice. "When we played Go, and you burnt your eyebrows. I was so happy that day. And I had that argument with Alison. I kept saying I liked everything in life equally and she wouldn't believe me, and all the time she was right. What I really meant was that you were the only thing that mattered and beyond that I didn't care about anything much at all."

'Don't tell me all this,' Patrick wanted to shout. 'For God's sake, have some human dignity.' Their roles had suddenly reversed, and instead of being the disciple, Patrick found he now had the power to inflict or withhold suffering as he chose. It was a terrifying godlike responsibility, to have another human being at his mercy. 'If you make yourself vulnerable to anyone,' Tyrone always said, 'they will punish you for it,' and he now knew what that meant. He realised he was just a thought away from despising Greg, not for making a pass at him, but for making him his confessor, for this display of self-abasement. It was as if Greg were a patient stripping off bandages one after another to reveal a gaping wound, and Patrick was being called upon to perform surgery when he could not even stand the sight of blood.

174

Greg was standing now. "I know I can trust you not to mention this to any of the Brothers." He was fiddling with his sleeve, pulling at a loose thread. "Brother Thomas will look after you while I am away on retreat, and when I come back it will be as if this never happened."

"But Greg." Patrick shook his head in disbelief. "Are you blind? I can't come back with you. I can never be a Brother now."

"Why?" There was a new note of panic in Greg's voice. "Nothing has changed."

"Everything has changed." How could he say that he had seen Greg as his mentor, and as such, Greg *was* the Brotherhood; that his failure in just one respect to live up to the standard had for Patrick invalidated the whole system. Just one microscopic crack was, in his eyes, sufficient to bring the whole structure crashing down. "And you must leave too," he went on. "My God, you're only human!" He wanted to seize Greg and shake him, but he had this irrational fear that he would disintegrate in his hands like a broken puppet.

"No." This was the old Greg: the politician. "I still believe in the way. My personal weaknesses can be overcome with determination. The road to enlightenment must involve some sacrifice," and he lay back on his mattress and closed his eyes. The mask was in place once more.

Patrick lay down too, knowing he would not sleep, and counted off the minutes until 5 a.m., when he fell asleep from sheer gaping exhaustion.

When he awoke, the bed next to him was empty. There was no sign of Greg downstairs or in the garden. He felt a combination of relief and sadness that he had been spared the necessity of saying goodbye. As he collected his few belongings together, he remembered the excitement and anticipation with which he had packed them, nearly two months before, and sensed himself spiralling downwards into a deep depression. The carrier bag he had originally used had long since disappeared, so he tucked his wallet and toothbrush inside the flute case, and tied his few clothes in a bundle with a piece of string. As he closed the door behind him and set off down the path towards the smoking chimneys in the distance, the faint sound of pan pipes came floating towards him from the misty stillness of the woods.

21

"CONGRATULATIONS," said Patrick.
    "Welcome back," said Alison.
"Here's to us," said Charlotte.
"Let's open another bottle," said Tyrone.

There was a bang and the tinkle of broken glass, as the champagne cork shot out of the bottle and hit the light-bulb above their heads, plunging the kitchen into darkness and showering the table with sharp fragments.

Fortunately, the meal was over. Alison and Patrick had tried to make a salmon pie in the shape of a fish, but the filling was too runny, and the pastry, over-buttery and disintegrating, refused to be sculpted. Eventually Charlotte came to their rescue, squashed the sticky mass into a flat loaf shape and wrote FISH across the top in pastry strips.

"There," she said, with an air of finality. "The power of the printed word will have to carry the day."

She, Alison and Tyrone had arranged to spend the weekend the results came out in Vanessa's holiday cottage at Birling Gap. This gathering had been planned during the brief period of post-exam euphoria, before the sense of anti-climax had set in, and was based injudiciously on the assumption that everyone would receive what they deserved at the hands of the examiners. Inevitably, this had turned out not to be the case. It had been Charlotte who had phoned the number which had been threatening to scorch a hole in her diary for the past five weeks. Predictably, she had been awarded a First, and she waited, biting her lip to hear the same of Alison. But when she had to relay to the anxious figure hopping up and down impatiently at her side the message of the anonymous voice, that Alison Laycott had been awarded a Lower Second, she felt a sort of helpless complicity with the examiners, as if it was she, Charlotte, who had decreed it.

Tyrone, on the other hand, was the recipient of an astounding piece of good fortune. Against all logic as Charlotte saw it, he too had been given a First. Even the awardee himself was incredulous, and for some minutes required strenuous reassurance that Charlotte was not playing a malicious trick on him.

The celebrations, which had been eagerly awaited, were abruptly suspended as Alison tremulously announced: "Congratulations, you two. I'm really happy for you," before bursting into tears and pounding upstairs to the bathroom. Charlotte and Tyrone followed sheepishly, to find she had locked herself in and could no more be enticed out by pleading than a limpet could be prised off a rock by rhetoric.

After half an hour of fruitless sympathy, they gave up, feeling guilty about their own success, and relieved that they had not been similarly penalised. The problem with denouncing the examiners as a bunch of incompetent geriatrics, Charlotte realised, was that it immediately challenged the validity of her own mark. And in that, surely, their judgement had been beyond reproach?

Tyrone was still dumbfounded by his unexpected and meteoric promotion to the company of the intellectual élite. His tutors would be outraged.

"I can't believe it," he told Charlotte, replacing the champagne in the fridge unopened. "I did get carried away during the exams, but I thought I'd left it too late to get even a respectable grade. I never took work seriously until ... until January, and then I couldn't concentrate properly because of ..." Sean's name hovered between them unspoken like a spectral presence.

Charlotte decided to risk it. "Sean would have been proud of you." It was the first time anyone had alluded directly to Sean, and she almost held her breath waiting for his reaction. 'What have I done?' she thought. 'Now I'll have two emotional wrecks on my hands instead of one.' But he just looked at her, and then beyond her into the middle distance, as if something was slowly dawning on him, before saying vaguely, "I'm just going for a walk," and disappearing out of the back door.

Charlotte wondered whether she had inadvertently precipitated a crisis, but decided that even if she had, it was better to have it out in the open at last. It was the suppression, the pregnant silences, that worried her. His departure also gave her the chance to comfort Alison alone. Tyrone's presence had been just another galling reminder of the arbitrariness of things. She braced herself mentally for the inevitable bombardment of ugly resentment, and then climbed the stairs, some ready words of sisterly commiseration on her lips.

Once Tyrone had escaped the house and its uneasy atmosphere, he felt more at liberty to indulge himself in the contemplation of his good news. He had not yet properly assimilated the idea that he, Tyrone, had received the highest grade the university could bestow. Every so often, distracted by a tiny bird bobbing along the verge beside him, or the sight of a field of long grass flattened by the wind like a shaggy coat, he would forget what it was he was so pleased about, then he would remember and an idiotic grin would spread over his face. He had never had this feeling before, of being undeservedly given a lucky break, being catapulted from the ranks of the unfortunate to those of the elect. He had never even won a raffle. It was a sign, he felt sure, and the mention of Sean's name had compounded the idea of the brightness of the present with the grimness of his recent past. He took the inland route rather than the half-mile tramp uphill to the top of the Seven Sisters. There would have been a good view out to sea, but he would save that for another time. He climbed over a mossy stile, slippery with recent rain, and into a broad and sloping field. He had a sense of something momentous coming upon him; an almost religious feeling of renewal; a chance to start again as a man with a future rather than a past. He needed to break his silence at last; to be forgiven. Patrick had always said Boris was the ideal person to tell one's problems to but Tyrone only knew Boris slightly — and anyway, he was miles away.

Tyrone was so engrossed in his thoughts that he was half-way across the field, entering a small ring of trees, before he realised he had become an object of some interest to a herd of cows. Tyrone was not afraid of cows in the irrational way certain people are afraid of spiders. He had come to a reasoned decision to fear them because they were large and heavy and unpredictable and could crush a man's skeleton like an eggshell if they felt like it.

As he stood there helplessly, the mighty creatures came lumbering towards him from all directions, fixing him with their glassy stares. He backed away as a couple stumbled heavily through the trees, twigs cracking under their hooves, but stopped abruptly as he saw that a solid line of the glaring animals had gathered behind him. He turned his head nervously, reluctant to make any sudden movements, and his scared gaze was met on all sides by a circle of implacable black and white faces. He was too frightened even to call out for help, fearing that an unexpected noise might trigger a stampede, but stood there, overcome by a creeping paralysis. The cows shuffled closer.

"Help," he whispered.

At last, after what seemed like hours of stalemate, the cows grew bored and began to amble off, leaving him free to make it to the edge of the field, where in his haste he slipped over and knelt in a cow-pat — the crowning indignity, he felt. When he arrived back at the cottage, breathless, sweating, and reeking of dung, he found Patrick had turned up unannounced, and was wandering around the house, flicking light switches on and off, and expounding the marvels of flush toilets.

The first thing Patrick had done on reaching a motorway service station, where he had been deposited by the last of a string of sympathetic motorists, was head for the canteen. In a calculated act of rebellion, he had opted for the stodgiest, most processed meal his finances could supply: a 'meat' pie (the menu declined to be more specific) and a long doughnut with what looked like a strip of cavity wall insulator and a trickle of jam down the middle. On the third mouthful of pie, the glutinous jelly, in which a few shrivelled peas were trapped like insects in amber, had already started to make him feel queasy. The pastry left a filmy coating all over his teeth. Disgusted, he chucked the remains in the bin and headed back to the roadside.

On his arrival at Oxford, he had been disappointed to find no sign of Alison, Charlotte or Tyrone. Then he remembered that term would have long since finished. A quick phone call to Vanessa Laycott had established their whereabouts, and a slightly longer trip to the bank had once again made public transport a viable option. It was from Vanessa, too, that Patrick learnt of Alison and Oliver's separation. The news filled him with surprise and anticipation. He recalled the last time he had seen her, in the High Street, fiddling with her engagement ring and looking edgy. That, he thought, had been the death knell for his chances. But now it looked as though there was a reprieve. He thought of the night in Boris's garden. With the futile clarity of hindsight, he could see that the covert antagonism between Greg and Alison had partly been on his account.

Alison and Charlotte were sitting on the front gate, hands in pockets, their feet hooked through the bars, when Patrick had appeared over the brow of the hill.

Charlotte's carefully chosen words of condolence and

support had succeeded in luring Alison out of the bathroom and a mood of bitterness and envy. At the cost of annulling her own success, Charlotte had preached the iniquities of the exam system as a measure of intelligence (a view she had always held in spite of it being to her advantage to believe otherwise).

As they sat there, the wind chapping their cheeks and glueing Alison's hair to her shiny lipstick, the distant hiker raised an arm in greeting. The two women peered over their shoulders down the lane to see who he was waving at, but there was no one else around.

"It's not Tyrone," Charlotte said, squinting into the sunlight, but before she could say any more, Alison gave a sudden cry of recognition, leapt off the gate and took off up the road, splashing through puddles, sending a spray of muddy flecks up the back of her legs.

As she watched the pair slither to a halt a few paces from one another and exchange some animated but inaudible conversation, Charlotte realised that the man she was looking at was Patrick.

"My God," she blurted out, as he approached the gate and gave her a bony squeeze, "what's happened to you? You look terrible."

It was only when Patrick saw Charlotte's shocked face that it occurred to him that he had not seen his reflection since that first day in Wales when he had peered into the water trough to see how Greg had cut his hair. Suddenly alarmed, he broke away from them and bolted indoors. He gave a start as he looked in the full-length mirror in the hall. The man he saw there was pathetically gaunt and skinny, with a jutting collarbone and prominent nose and cheekbones, accentuated by shorn hair, which had only regrown sufficiently to look uneven. There were brown crescents under his eyes and he had twenty-four hours of blond stubble. It struck him that he looked more like Greg than himself. It was not a comfortable thought.

By the time they had eaten dinner, drunk a toast and picked the pieces of glass out of the fruit bowl, Patrick had given his friends a brief account of life under the Brotherhood's regime. He avoided any reference to Greg's declaration and the real reason for his departure, saying instead that he found the lifestyle too austere. He knew that this would make him seem feeble and dilettantish, and confirm their opinion that he was just a dabbler, but he was prepared to bear that much at least for Greg's sake.

"It was all right for the others," he rambled. "They all believe in a God of sorts, but all I believed in was the Brotherhood, and when I found that it was not everything I wanted it to be, it all fell apart. By the way, how is your tramp?" he asked Alison, trying to steer the subject away from himself.

Alison looked down at her hands. She still felt a niggling sense of failure about the Archie affair — not so much because he had died, but because he had broken her trust and abused her clumsy attempts at kindness. He would have apologised, she felt sure, if only he had lived.

"He's dead," she told him. "Broke into the Women's Refuge, stole a bottle of whisky, got drunk and fell down a flight of steps."

"Oh dear," said Patrick, who had not been expecting anything quite so final.

Tyrone squirmed. "He didn't exactly fall," he said slowly, not quite catching anyone's eye. "I pushed him." There was an atmosphere in the room so electric that it almost crackled.

"What?" Alison's voice was dangerously quiet.

"It was an accident," he stammered on, as Charlotte and Patrick looked up, open-mouthed. "He tried to rough me up as I was walking along the alley, so I pushed him out of the way and he fell . . ."

"I can't believe what I'm hearing," Alison stormed, all her anger and resentment at his undeserved success suddenly finding a legitimate focus. "You just left him dying? You bloody thug. How could you? And never told anyone, or went for help? Christ. He was a person not just a pile of rags." Tyrone had suddenly metamorphosed in her mind into a symbol of everything that was thwarting her. Still ranting, she picked up a plate and threw it past his head so it shattered on the wall behind him, making him flinch, then she stalked out, banging the door.

Charlotte, completely taken aback by the confession and its consequences, excused herself and chased after Alison, scared by her uncharacteristic display of violence.

In the kitchen, Patrick looked at the bowed head of Tyrone across the table. He shifted on his seat, deeply embarrassed and uncomfortable. If only he had gone after Alison, it would have given him the chance to be alone with her and spared him the torment of sitting there, groping for the appropriate words. The silence was dense and threatening — it threatened him with the inevitability that it would soon be broken. He rose to his feet, preparing to slip out (I'm a coward, he thought), when Tyrone looked up, a dark and desperate expression on his face, and said seriously, "Don't go. There's something I must say. I can't keep it to myself any longer or I'll go mad."

Patrick was seized by a sense of impending doom. It was as if he had heard it all before. 'Tyrone is going to tell me he loves me,' he thought hysterically. Reluctantly, almost mesmerised, he sat down again.

"He didn't fall. I killed him."

Patrick let out a breath like the last hiss of air escaping from a balloon. "I know. I heard. You couldn't help it." He had not even worked out what he felt about Tyrone's part in Archie's death. It was the secrecy of the whole thing that had shocked him.

"Not him," he heard Tyrone saying. He heard it quite distinctly but it took him a long time to make sense of the words. "Sean."

"Sean?" Patrick tried to wake himself up. 'This is a nightmare. Any minute I'll wake up,' he thought.

"I cut the rope . . . I cut it myself with a knife." He began to drone on as if he had rehearsed the story again and again, looking past Patrick's shoulder and out of the window into the darkness. Every word made Patrick contract with horror. He felt as though his whole body had become a giant ear,

184

forced against its will to hear something unspeakable.

"We were roped together. I was leading, putting runners in as I went to secure the rope to the rock. There was an overhang jutting out, and I'd gone diagonally across it and belayed on this ledge. It was a freezing cold day, the coldest I've ever known. Sean started to follow, but when he got about half-way to the last nut, he slipped and it came right out, and he swung out into space about fifteen feet below me, just hanging there. It was my fault for not protecting it properly.

"There was no way he could reach the rock face, and the ropes stretch, so I couldn't pull him up. We stayed like that for seven hours. We screamed for help until we were hoarse but no one came. Then it started to get dark. He'd been calling up to me "Don't leave me," as if I could — we were roped together. I had to brace myself against the rock the whole time to stop the weight of him dragging me over. Then he went quiet. I sat it out as long as I could. Then it started to get cold. So cold I couldn't speak; my lips felt huge and clumsy. I thought I was going to die of hypothermia. I started to hallucinate. I don't know what made me think of using my pen-knife, but once the thought had wormed its way into my mind, I couldn't get it out again. I thought, 'If I don't do it we're both going to die anyway.' At about three in the morning I took it out. It took me an hour to get it open; my hands were that cold. Then I reached down the ledge and started to cut. I don't know whether he'd passed out earlier, but he suddenly looked up and saw me trying to cut through it. I can't forget the way he looked at me. 'What are you doing?' he said, but I kept on sawing away. It wasn't a quick clean cut — the knife was blunt. All I could think of was *what if he survived knowing what I'd done*. Then he screamed a sort of whimpering scream, and I shut my eyes."

There was a pause.

"He was my best friend and I let him fall."

Patrick found himself staring intently at a spider on the fridge. His heart was thumping against his ribs so hard it felt like a football being kicked around a cage. Tyrone was silent.

Patrick couldn't look at him. He knew a response was expected, a reaction required. He realised he had become a surrogate Sean, with the power to condemn or forgive, and that Tyrone was waiting. But he felt numb, drained, and suddenly terribly tired of other people and their unwholesome secrets. He tried to concentrate, to manufacture some appropriate emotion — disbelief, or pity, or shock, to give Tyrone the relief he was craving. Words flitted through his mind, but there was a degree of abstraction about them all. None of them expressed what he really felt; the weariness, the reluctance to play God, to expend any more emotion. So he just sat there, watching the spindly movements of the spider, until Tyrone stood up, knocking the chair backwards, and blundered out of the room.

Charlotte, who had just come downstairs having run a hot bath for Alison, was puzzled by the silence, and was hovering behind the kitchen door, when Tyrone came bursting out, nearly knocking her off her feet.

"Charlotte," he said, grabbing hold of her in the way that a drunk might fall against a tree. Charlotte shrank back. While talking to Alison about Archie, she had been doing some silent calculations. Tyrone must have killed Archie the same night he had made love to her. The idea left a bitter taste in her mouth. It was macabre. As if getting pregnant had not been bad enough, this new development made her feel thoroughly soiled. If only he had told her, she would have been able to help him sort it out and she certainly wouldn't have fallen into bed with him the way she had. It was with these thoughts still on her mind that she shrugged his arms off firmly. He flopped back on to her, pawing at her shirt.

"I hate myself," he was saying. "Everything I touch ..." he struggled for a word, "... dies." He buried his head in her neck. Charlotte could feel a rivulet of sweat dripping down her cleavage. All she could think was, 'I've been here before, with him holding me like this. This is how it all started before,' and with a nauseous feeling in her stomach she remembered the hospital waiting room, the sickening smell of the operating theatre and the searing humiliation of being conscious during the whole procedure. She recoiled, unable to comfort him. "Don't be melodramatic," she said impatiently, full of self-pity. "You aren't the only person in the world who has ever suffered."

He swayed for a second, without her arms to support him, and clutched at the banisters. "What do you mean?"

She had not wanted to get too specific. "I mean," she hesitated slightly, "other people feel guilty about things too ..."

"Like what exactly? What other people? Do you mean you? What things?" He had sensed something confessional in her tone, something that indicated she was not talking generalities, and he was not to be put off.

"Don't force me to tell you," she pleaded. "You won't want to know." But this merely had the effect of exciting him even more.

"What? What?" he demanded, digging his fingers into her arm. Perhaps he was not alone. Perhaps she too had seen the beast in man.

"I had an abortion."

For a minute he thought she was referring to an event in her distant past, and then it hit him, like a stinging slap on the face. She meant his child.

"Why didn't you tell me?" He was still reeling.

"What good would it have done?"

"I could have helped."

This made her laugh bitterly. How could a man 'help' when it was always, always the woman who had to take the responsibility, to bear the humiliation, the guilt, the pain.

"I would have paid," he began.

"We could have gone Dutch. How modern," she interrupted sarcastically.

He was no longer weak and hysterical, but quiet and thoughtful instead. She could feel him withdrawing from her inside himself. He seemed to be working something out, wrestling so hard with some mental problem that his eyes glazed over. For a moment she thought he was going to have a fit, but then, without another word, he walked right past her and out of the front door, which the wind caught and flung shut with a tremendous crash.

A couple of hours after she had crept upstairs to bed, Charlotte was awakened by a loud banging. The noise had incorporated itself into her dream, and she sat up, disorientated for a moment, before realising that her bedroom door, which did not shut properly, was rattling against the frame. The wind was shrieking outside, beating the windows and making the tin roof vibrate and groan. Slipping out of bed, Charlotte fumbled for the light switch. Nothing. She tried the bedside lamp. That too was dead. The banging was getting on her nerves. She jiggled the door handle; then, when that failed, stuffed a magazine between the bottom of the door and the carpet. The gale was still raging outside and, drawing the curtains, Charlotte could see lines of trees in the nearby coppice bucking and diving like wild animals. As she watched, one of them came crashing to the ground, its roots torn up and exposed like a deformed fist.

There was not a single light to be seen as far as the horizon. The power lines were down. It was an eerie, reluctant darkness. Charlotte remembered her parents' stories of the blackouts. Every so often a small, mean, punctured football of a moon became visible through a break in the clouds. At the end of the garden another tree went over with a wrenching noise and struck an abandoned car, stoving the roof in as though it were made of foil. 'Tyrone can't have stayed out in this,' she told herself. Stuffing cotton wool in her ears and strapping a pair of socks over them with a headscarf, she managed to muffle the noise of the storm to a dull booming. Wishing she could stifle her imagination as easily, she drifted into a disturbed sleep.

Charlotte was not the only one having trouble sleeping.

Patrick, still fully dressed, was standing by his window

abstractedly watching sections of the shed roof peel off like damp wallpaper and blow down the lane.

He was still trying to assimilate what Tyrone had told him, but found his thoughts wandering again and again to Alison and his own problems. Circumstances seemed to have conspired to prevent him being alone with her. As he stood there, the remaining portion of roof rose and sank a couple of times like a mouth gasping for air, before lifting off and being tossed into the adjoining garden, flattening a large section of fence. Patrick sighed; that would have to be patched up in the morning. He was wondering how the others could possibly be sleeping through the noise when there was a faint tap at the door.

Alison stood there, dwarfed by a man's checked dressing gown, her face pale from recent crying.

"The lights have all gone out," she said.

"It's the storm," Patrick said stupidly. "Look at the shed."

She crossed over to the window which was flexing dangerously, the wind nearly sucking it out of the frame. The shed, its innards exposed to reveal a tangle of garden implements, bicycles and hosepiping, looked horribly intestinal.

She grimaced. "What a mess."

"Yes."

"I mean, everything."

"Yes."

Patrick knew he sounded like a robot. Why was it, he wondered, that with all his linguistic training, his exhaustive study of the riches of two languages, at the crucial moments of his life he always became so agonisingly monosyllabic.

"You're still dressed. Haven't you been to bed?" Alison asked, noticing his jeans and shirt which in the gloom she had mistaken for pyjamas.

"No. I can't sleep. I feel wide awake." He wanted her to look at him, but she was gazing out of the window. Somewhere in the distance a light flickered on, and then another, a pair of fiery eyes sparkling in the gloom. Looking down, Patrick noticed that he was wearing odd socks. They weren't even remotely similar.

Suddenly a dustbin came bowling through the gap in the fence, and was whipped up in the air as if it was nothing more than a paper cup. Rubbish was blowing around like confetti.

Then it came to him — the one perfect innocent word. "Well ..." he said, staring straight at her.

Alison looked up warily, and then, as the word tugged at a loose thread somewhere in her memory, she gave a smile of recognition.

"Come here," she said.

※

The next morning, before Charlotte, Patrick and Alison were awake, a group of children were walking along the beach below the cliffs.

"Race you to that log," shouted the eldest, a boy of eight, already breaking away from the rest of his companions, who set up plaintive cries of protest before scampering after him.

But as he grew closer, he could see that the log was not a log, and he skittered to a halt on the shingle.

"What is it?" a fair-haired girl began, and then stopped, as the rest of the group came straggling up. The youngest, a two-year-old, did not stop when she reached the little knot of anxious figures, but kept waddling on towards the strange object.

"Asleep," she gurgled, prodding it.

"Come away from there," said the older boy sharply, running up and pulling her away by the sleeve. Taking command, he ushered the little group along the beach, occasionally giving a furtive glance behind him at the body half impacted in the shale, and the seagulls whirling and screeching above it.

22

A fortnight after the funeral, Patrick sat perched on the piano stool in the Time Room absent-mindedly writing his name in the dust on the lid. The clocks whirred and ticked in the background. It was so long since he had last been there, he could not remember which one actually told the correct time. 'It doesn't matter anyway,' he thought; he had nothing to hurry for. The sun was bouncing off the grimy window panes, making them look opaque, bringing to life beams of glowing dust particles. Caught there in the light they looked so dense that Patrick decided Boris's lungs must be coated with a thick growth of lint like a hoover bag.

Uncle Solly, in the corner, was in need of water. The bottom leaf had turned brown and dropped off into the pot, and the tip of a new one, pale green and tightly curled, poked discreetly from the top. There was a brown stain on the carpet by his feet caused, Patrick remembered, by Boris knocking the coffee over that day, his twenty-first birthday, when Boris had first played him Patrick's Song. He could use Blitz on it, he thought grimly. That day seemed a whole lifetime ago now; a day in the life of a different Patrick.

He could hear Boris talking in the next room. He had only just stepped over the threshold when Boris had been called to the phone. Patrick had closed the dividing door out of courtesy, but it would have made no difference if he had hovered at Boris's elbow. He was talking in Polish.

Patrick wandered over to the desk. A sheet of paper was protruding from the typewriter, embossed with braille pimples. He stroked them blankly. Incredible, he thought, that a vague scratching sensation on the fingertips could, to someone in the know, actually yield up a message. It was the ultimate in close reading. He wondered if a shiver ever ran up Boris's arm when he read something moving. Imagine feeling one's way through Keats. It had just occurred to him that to make any sense of Boris, with his clocks, braille, Esperanto and Polish, one needed to be a sort of code-breaker, when there was a click of a receiver being replaced, and Boris re-appeared, smiling broadly.

"My younger brother, Jan, in Toronto," he explained. "His wife has just given birth to a son. They are calling it Boris after me." He chuckled. "Now I suppose I will have to think of an appropriate gift. What might Boris Gutkin junior require on his journey through life?"

"You could compose a song for him," Patrick suggested drily, looking at Boris's face to see if there was any reaction. The issue of Patrick's Song, and its ignominious fate, had been weighing on his conscience for over two months now. He noticed Boris's lips twitching. "You know, don't you?" he said accusingly. Boris's faced relaxed into a smile.

"I must confess I do not often listen to commercial radio stations, but it so happened some weeks ago Ilsa left the radio on in the kitchen, and try as I might, I could not turn the wretched machine off. Blitz stain remover. Very good. Yes." He seemed to find the whole thing a huge joke. "At first I thought it was a monstrous coincidence, that my song had simultaneously been composed by someone else. It worried me. I thought, 'perhaps every tune that it is possible to write has already been written, and there are no more combinations left.'" He beamed at Patrick. "Imagine my relief when I received a letter saying my entry had won second prize in a radio competition, accompanied by fifty pounds and the promise of twenty-four bottles of the relevant detergent."

Patrick cringed. He had forgotten that he had put Boris's address on the entry form.

"I'm so sorry. I didn't realise it was an advertising jingle they were after. I don't know why I did it anyway. Please forgive me."

Boris waved this away with a dismissive gesture. "Of course, of course. But," he went on, "do you know the ultimate villainy? It doesn't work."

"What?" Patrick was forced to smile himself now.

"Ilsa tried it on the carpet. She tells me however hard you rub, it still leaves a mark."

"Oh dear," said Patrick helplessly.

"But enough of this," he groped for one of Patrick's bony hands and took it between his own. Patrick looked down at them, embarrassed. He had never noticed before how large Boris's hands were. They were enormous, and freckled, with long fingers and knuckles like chestnuts.

"I'm so sorry about Tyrone. Poor boy." He shook his head and gave a sigh which made the chair vibrate.

The story of the brilliant student who had accidentally fallen to his death the day he had received first-class honours from Oxford had briefly made the tabloid press.

"It was suicide," Patrick said simply.

Boris stiffened, tightening his grip on Patrick's hand. "Go on," he said evenly.

"He was my best friend and I let him down."

"Are you sure it was suicide? Would his parents not have suspected something?"

"No. Tyrone had been harbouring this secret — something he had done which he couldn't live with. He appealed to us for help, and we all, in one way or another, failed him. His mother came to see me. He was her only child — her husband died five years ago. She was older than I imagined. Tyrone must have been a bit of an autumn crocus." There was the faintest crack in his voice. "I'll never forget her. She was wearing a cream-coloured summer suit with a stain on the lapel. She had tried to cover it up with a brooch, but you could still see it. And she was tiny. She had make-up on — not really bright and awful like some old women, but just neat and nice, as if she didn't want to let him down in front of his friends. She didn't stay long. She wanted to know if we knew of any reason why he might have wanted to commit suicide — if we were as sure as the police that it had been an accident. What could I say without betraying his secret? I mean, he was her only son. All she would have of him now would be memories. So I said he had been happy on that last day. Excited about his exam result. Looking forward to the future. She seemed relieved. Do you think I did wrong?"

Boris had released his hand. "If only life was merely a matter of choosing between right and wrong," he said, but Patrick was barely listening.

"I've always tried to do the right thing," he was saying. "If only there was a formula. That was all I wanted from the Brotherhood. A formula that worked."

Boris traced the outline of his lips thoughtfully with one finger. "It's not finding the formula that's important," he said. "It's the seeking. All the time you are being seduced by a new system like the Brotherhood" (Patrick winced at the metaphor) "you are receptive to the idea of change. But the moment you accept its code as absolute, you stop thinking about it, you stop challenging yourself. It's a little like this autobiography business. The moment you think you have a word or phrase which expresses exactly what you want to say, without any falsification, and you commit it to paper, the meaning instantly seems to drain away." As if struck by a thought, he moved away to his desk and slowly typed a few words. "Even so," he smiled, "one limps on."

"How is it going — the book?" Patrick asked. "How did you solve the problem of your mother?"

"Ah, that. By renouncing the idea of a solution. Every word I write is still a mere ghost of what I feel, but I press on, inspired and frustrated by turns. After all, the alternative is nothingness. Oblivion." He ran his hands over the top sheet and smiled, as though he had just read something witty. "And you? What are your plans for your doctorate?"

"That's all over. Perhaps I'll pick it up again one day. I'm not living in Oxford any more. I'm staying with Alison in her mother's flat in London, until we find jobs. We've got a bit of a thing going. You'll have to come and see us when we're settled."

"What jobs?"

"Alison may work for her mother on the magazine for a while. I'm thinking of museums. myself " He stood up to leave, giving Boris's hand a tug.

"And is this love, this thing you have going?" Boris enquired innocently, batting Patrick's own idiom back at him.

Patrick shrugged. "I don't know what you'd call it. It's something," he added over his shoulder as he set off down the path. "It gets us through the day."

The same day, Charlotte received her degree from the Chancellor of the University. There had once been a tacit expectation that the three of them, she, Alison and Tyrone, would all graduate together. But Alison, still disappointed with her result, had lost interest in the place, and had decided not to bother.

"But you worked for three years for that piece of paper," Charlotte protested. "You surely don't think it was all a waste of time?"

Although Charlotte was ideologically suspicious of ceremony, she nursed a guilty affection for the ritualistic clobber that went with an Oxford degree. She despised herself for her sentimentality, for feeling that some form of public gesture was the appropriate way to round things off neatly, and then tried to convince herself she was doing it for her parents.

So she had put on her black skirt — the same one she had worn to Tyrone's funeral (it still smelled of furniture polish and pipe-smoke) and her gown and hat as solemnly as a nun, and her parents sat in the audience, almost bursting out of their new outfits with pride.

Outside on the forecourt, Charlotte was enveloped in a

sticky embrace by a perspiring Mrs Rowley, who had already started to shed layers of clothing, and had spent most of the ceremony scraping a ragged tissue around her face and cleavage. Crowds of pink-faced graduates were fanning themselves with mortarboards. Women in high heels were walking unsteadily across the gravel. Inside the theatre the atmosphere had throbbed with self-congratulation. To Charlotte, the whole place seemed to drip with an unbearable smugness. As she emerged, a large, heavily made-up woman behind her was gesticulating with a cigarette and saying to her son in a ringing voice, "This is the proudest day of my life."

But as soon as they were disgorged into the open air, the aura of confidence evaporated quicker than the sweat on the back of the men's necks. People were hovering around aimlessly. Slight acquaintances kept accosting Charlotte and asking her where Alison was. Nobody mentioned Tyrone. Through a gap in the crowd, she spotted Oliver surrounded by a little knot of acolytes. He caught Charlotte's eye and elbowed his way through the throng towards her. She smiled nervously. He always made her uneasy; it was something to do with the vampiric way he demanded female sympathy. Merely conversing with him was not enough. She knew he would not be content until he had drained her of everything, leaving her a dried up husk. It would also be difficult to avoid alluding to Alison, who was, after all, the only thing they had in common.

"Hello, Charlotte," he said briskly. He was wearing a casual shirt and brightly coloured tie, with black jeans, but in spite of the outfit he seemed to have aged in the couple of months since Alison had left him.

Charlotte looked around to introduce her parents, but they had retreated to a discreet distance.

"Hello, Oliver."

"Congratulations on your result. Excellent." He nodded vigorously.

"Thank you." She was determined not to simper.

"What are you going to do with it, is the question. The

world's your oyster, of course, someone like you. Young ..." he hesitated, "... attractive. What's that bit from Dickens? 'The mists had all solemnly risen now, and the world lay spread before me.'" He sounded wistful — almost envious.

Before Charlotte could reply, one of his harem had detached herself from the group and tapped him on the shoulder.

"Oliver, we're going for a drink now. Are you coming?"

He expanded like a flower.

"Oh yes. Just coming." He turned back to Charlotte. "Well, goodbye, and all the best."

Charlotte felt a stab of pity for him. "And to you too," and she tugged his proffered hand. "By the way," she said, "I like your tie."

"Oh, do you?" he said, enormously gratified. "I'm so pleased." And she watched him stroll across the road to the pub, still fingering his tie delightedly.

Her parents rejoined her. "What now?" Mrs Rowley asked.

Charlotte did not feel ready to leave. She did not want this to be her last memory of the place, standing in the midst of a shifting throng of people who seemed certain at that moment of nothing beyond their own excellence.

"Do you mind if I go off on my own for a few minutes?" she asked, as they wove their way to the perimeter of the crowd.

It was cooler walking. She felt her gown billowing out behind her as she ran, so she took it off and rolled it into a bundle, and stuffed her hat into her waistband. She did not stop until she reached the river, which was black and rippling in the breeze, breaking up the sunlight into tiny flakes of metal. She stood on the bridge looking over, thinking. So many of her thoughts lately seemed to start with the words 'if only ...' and thoughts like that were lousy company. Tyrone was free of that anyway. 'You jumped,' she addressed him silently, 'but we have all fallen.' It occurred to her fleetingly that guilt was a form of energy — never destroyed, only transferred. Perhaps between the three of them, it had been sufficiently dissipated to be manageable.

197

The breeze was stronger by the river. Down on the bank she recognised the figure of Boris, trying to feed a large and noisy group of ducks. Each time he threw out a chunk of bread, the wind would blow it straight back at him, pinning it to the front of his whiskery coat. The ducks, feathers ruffling, were struggling against the gusts to paddle towards him. Smiling obliviously, Boris continued to toss out pieces of bread until the bag he was holding was empty, and the front of his coat matted with crumbs.

Charlotte went to wave, then remembered, and turning away, headed back up the hill, chin up, straining against the wind.

Discover more about our forthcoming books through Penguin's FREE newspaper...

Penguin
Quarterly

It's packed with:

- exciting features
- author interviews
- previews & reviews
- books from your favourite films & TV series
- exclusive competitions & much, much more...

Write off for your free copy today to:
Dept JC
Penguin Books Ltd
FREEPOST
West Drayton
Middlesex
UB7 0BR
NO STAMP REQUIRED

READ MORE IN PENGUIN

In every corner of the world, on every subject under the sun, Penguin represents quality and variety – the very best in publishing today.

For complete information about books available from Penguin – including Puffins, Penguin Classics and Arkana – and how to order them, write to us at the appropriate address below. Please note that for copyright reasons the selection of books varies from country to country.

In the United Kingdom: Please write to *Dept. JC, Penguin Books Ltd, FREEPOST, West Drayton, Middlesex UB7 OBR*

If you have any difficulty in obtaining a title, please send your order with the correct money, plus ten per cent for postage and packaging, to *PO Box No. 11, West Drayton, Middlesex UB7 OBR*

In the United States: Please write to *Penguin USA Inc., 375 Hudson Street, New York, NY 10014*

In Canada: Please write to *Penguin Books Canada Ltd, 10 Alcorn Avenue, Suite 300, Toronto, Ontario M4V 3B2*

In Australia: Please write to *Penguin Books Australia Ltd, 487 Maroondah Highway, Ringwood, Victoria 3134*

In New Zealand: Please write to *Penguin Books (NZ) Ltd,182–190 Wairau Road, Private Bag, Takapuna, Auckland 9*

In India: Please write to *Penguin Books India Pvt Ltd, 706 Eros Apartments, 56 Nehru Place, New Delhi 110 019*

In the Netherlands: Please write to *Penguin Books Netherlands B.V., Keizersgracht 231 NL–1016 DV Amsterdam*

In Germany: Please write to *Penguin Books Deutschland GmbH, Friedrichstrasse 10–12, W–6000 Frankfurt/Main 1*

In Spain: Please write to *Penguin Books S. A., C. San Bernardo 117–6° E–28015 Madrid*

In Italy: Please write to *Penguin Italia s.r.l., Via Felice Casati 20, I–20124 Milano*

In France: Please write to *Penguin France S. A., 17 rue Lejeune, F–31000 Toulouse*

In Japan: Please write to *Penguin Books Japan, Ishikiribashi Building, 2–5–4, Suido, Bunkyo-ku, Tokyo 112*

In Greece: Please write to *Penguin Hellas Ltd, Dimocritou 3, GR–106 71 Athens*

In South Africa: Please write to *Longman Penguin Southern Africa (Pty) Ltd, Private Bag X08, Bertsham 2013*

BY THE SAME AUTHOR

Back Trouble

'Charming . . . A funny and moving story with a great deal of style' – *Sunday Telegraph*

On the brink of forty, newly single with a failed business, Philip thought he'd reached an all-time low. It only needed a discarded chip on a South London street to lay him literally flat.

So, bed-bound and bored, Philip naturally starts to write the story of his life but reveals more surprises, both comic and touching, than Philip or his family ever bargained for. Even, perhaps, a happy ending . . .

'This is a funny book which slips in some acute and painful observations on the side' – *The Times*